She Changes

TERESSA MARK

She

Changes

A Goddess Myth for Modern Women

 Delphi Press, Inc. Oak Park, Illinois

© 1991 by Teressa Mark

Published 1991 by Delphi Press Inc., Oak Park, IL.
All rights reserved.

No parts of this book may be reproduced in any form, except for brief quotations accompanying reviews in newspapers or magazines, without the prior written consent of the publisher.

ISBN 1-878980-03-3
Library of Congress Catalog Number: 91-71137

96 95 94 93 92 91   6 5 4 3 2 1

The paper used in this publication meets the minimum requirements of American National Standard for Information Sciences—Permanence of Paper for Printed Library Materials, ANSI Z39.48-1984.

Starhawk's chant, "She Changes" from *Dreaming the Dark* ©1982, 1988 by Miriam Simos. Used by permission of Beacon Press.

To my brother

"If only we would let ourselves

be dominated as things do

by some immense storm

we would become strong too,

and not need names"

Ranier Marie Rilke

CHAPTER 1

It took me awhile to accommodate myself to the fact that the groom was a ghost, but I said my "I do's" and it was no problem when no one reciprocated. I was thirteen years old and was dreaming.

Today is my wedding day. I am marrying The Ghost. An hour from now I will put on the habit of a religious and lie prostrate in the center aisle of the monastery church. I am 39 years old, I have had the longest postulancy on record. I have been "on hold" as they say. The community eyes you, you eye yourself . . . life is full of ayes and nays . . . and too much levity.

The first time I received a calling down on this aspect of my personality I thought of Kerb Ball. You must curb it, the Novice Mistress said, and my whole psyche turned with all the other kids on the block, to watch his ball hit the street corner as if it were the tip of the Great Pyramid. POW! We were convinced you had to be Jewish to play the best damn ball on Amsterdam Avenue.

"Sister Mark, will you please hold still! My, you're hot! must be the satin." Two pins, plucked from between Sister Reginald's thin lips, disappear into a fold gathered at my waist. "There, no one will notice."

"All done." A gentle voice and a tug on the arm I hold outright into the room, pulls my eyes to Sister Barnabas and her handiwork. Thirty seedling pearl buttons, shiny collars closed, march upright from my wrist to my elbow. Her simple joy in being allowed to help Sister Reginald, who manfully and peremptorily takes all responsibility for the outfitting of new brides, is contagious. "You look beautiful!" she says.

"Internal beauty's what's important," Sister Reginald mutters the words to the long satin train.

I smile at Barney's flushed face over Reginald's back, "Shall I go and get the veil?" she asks.

"It's not going to come to us on its own."

Squeezing my hand, she leaves. Some minutes pass before Sister Reginald, stopping, sits back on her heels.

"The veil will hide the gathers . . . Mrs. Andrews is, to say the least, buxom." 'Bux' comes out with an explosive pop. It was considered a blessing to have your wedding gown used by one of the sisters and as a result, we had closetsful of gowns.

"But you, Sister Mark," she looks at me as if a toad has gotten trapped in the ciborium, "well, it will not matter. You're ready, as ready as ever you'll be. I'll go get Reverend Mother."

A breeze comes through the tall windows catching the celebratory lace panels, carrying them forward like searching fingers. I watch the woman in the bridal gown with the shoulder length, dark brown hair. In the full length mirror brought down from the attic, the fresh air buoys the cream and blue linens and lace over her head. The stark cell has been transformed into a bower out of Arabian Nights; the twelve-foot-high ceiling, hidden, the cloth moves ever so gently.

Deflected from rising, the air divides. On either side of the plank bed and straw mattress, it plays with the ribbon bouquets fastened to the wall by the novices. The gaily colored strands dance every which way, over the rough grey wool blanket; one thin curl of pink, reaching farther than the rest, hovers over the water basin, escapes the enervating spirit, falls, and does not rise again.

I think of my parents sitting in the front pew of the

church, the great curtain lowered so they can watch the ceremony. I don't think I've been successful in explaining, "what a good Irish girl would want to go and do this for."

If there hadn't been so many of us. If, searching for peace and quiet, I hadn't started hanging out in churches.

When Mother caught on that I was not visiting Sally, Suzie and Diane, and forbade me to go to church except on Sundays, it was too late. The braided gold had turned over at the base of my spine. A sentinel, a cobra, it stretched, yawned and slept no more.

I carried it like a turd. I didn't want it. I wanted to be a young girl and do all the things that young girls do. It interfered with everything, nothing weighed beside it!

I stopped running the day I walked up to the monastery door and rang the buzzer.

"Talking to yourself about buzzers, hummn . . . you're thinking buzzers and I'm thinking shoes, there are no white shoes, you know. Still . . ." her voice is thoughtful, "quite a few have walked to the altar in their bare feet."

The little doubting core at the center of my being relaxes as I turn to Reverend Mother Damian of Mary. All six foot three of her stands just inside the door.

She holds a three foot long pascal candle festooned with enormous, white calla lilies. Their centers are too gaping, too golden, they are obscene in their realism. I look away, at the mass of white tulle fastened to the slim gold band riding on Mother's shoulder like a foxtail stole, but, my eyes are pulled back to those callas.

"I'm going to carry those?"

"Sister?"

"Well . . . I mean . . . Mother?"

"Sister Timothy went to great pains."

I love her, I trust her. She was the one who swung the vote that finally allowed me in. She is the one who knows the fire curls higher year by year. "They remind me of Aaron and his flaming rod, no disrespect, Mother!" I drop on my knees, the heavy fabric folds around me, and kiss her hand.

She sighs, "I provoked that. You're ready, I hear," the firm hands help me rise. Graciously, she does not repeat the remainder of Sister Reginald's announcement. "Let me look at you. Sister has outdone herself tucking and tightening, hasn't she?"

A retort comes to me but I am learning to keep my mouth shut.

"We will not cut your hair as you will be leaving for school." She makes it sound as if I will be missed, God bless her!

"Remember, stay down for the entire Te Deum."

"Yes."

"No fussing around on the floor."

She is referring to those who cannot bear their nose turning into a woody thing without scratching. No futzing, no mussing, we ain't got time for cussing . . . oh . . . oh. Unconsciously a soft-shoe routine grabs at my stocking feet. I pull my toes primly side by side and grin.

Mother Damian's eyes search me as if zeroing in on the silent inhabitant, the one hidden in the back room.

A cloaked heaviness settles on the long hall outside the cell. The community gathers, they wear the ceremonial habits and flowing choir mantles, and the effect is a weighing down and hushing of the old creaky floorboards.

Someone starts chanting the "Salve Regina." My eyes fill with tears of happiness as Reverend Mother places the slender crown on my hair, fluffing the veil about my shoulders.

From their pews on the other side of the floor to ceiling grill faces strain to devour me; I grin and wave, trying to lighten the atmosphere.

I kneel for a long time. A token brown curl is cut and falls limply on the parqueted floor. I say some words. Finally, I leave the church to remove the bridal finery; I'll never forget the weight of the habit as it falls.

Lying prone on the hard floor, arms outstretched, body in the form of a cross, Reverend Mother Damian and Mother Sub-Prioress scurry above me making sure I'm decent. The choir mantle is pulled as close to my fingertips as it will go, the coarse material of the habit adjusted along both achilles tendons.

Sister Sacristan sets the register higher than usual, "Te Deum Laudamus" . . . I know it by heart. My soul swells with gratitude, I have found my place, my work, my life!

At the words "Holy Ghost" Sister Dolores activates the chimes in the choir campanile. Constructed asymmetrically, all the frequencies come into play. Overtones and fundamentals elbow the bony sections of my head. The intervals widen. I, and my skull, assume a different spatial arrangement, a real dynamic range.

Dual pitch moves circular-wise at the base of my spine, a fakir drawing the hooded one from hiding. Bonaparte was in a runaway carriage that he believed himself to be driving. I know I am not driving. I have absolutely no control of this. I am too full of joy to care.

A lonely majestic tone full of particles, wavers and cries for kind. Each tone attenuates quickly, but I am left with residual wavelengths of light. These pulse vehemently as the door opens and the liquid gold one begins to climb.

"Sister!" the whisper is insistent, "you must rise now." Hands on either side, I am drawn up feeling weak and unsteady. There is a hole in the middle of my forehead, I can feel it. But no, when I reach up I find the skin unbroken. It throbs but it is unbroken.

"Tell me what happened."

I keep my voice low and steady, "You mean in choir?"

There is no mincing around the pointedness of the manner in which she sits, hands folded on the rough grey cloth of her scapula, facing me.

"It moved higher." Reverend Mother is absolutely still. "The bells left their safe range, it became very intense." A sigh escapes me, remembering.

"The Te Deum became so much more than the single monody we know it as," I searched for words, "it became, it became like trading fours, Reverend Mother, you know, with all the improvisation, alternating, responding to each other's thought."

She isn't helping me at all. I realize my garbled account is less than adequate. "The energy rose up to my chest as usual. Then, after what seemed like some sort of call and response with the universe, during which my bony frame dissolved, it roared up my neck and out my forehead."

There! I try for lightness, "not out the top of my head like the books say."

She does not smile. "How do you feel?"

"I, I feel great. I feel right, somehow," I shrug, my shoulders and the unfamiliar, lovely weight of the toque and veil register, "I feel very good, Mother."

For long moments she sits looking at me, and then for equally long moments focuses down as if carrying on a silent conversation with her hands.

"The only person who has the wits to know you're not possessed by a devil is three hundred miles away, I'll give you his name, he's in a small obscure Camaldolese monastery in the western part of the state. I want you to promise me you'll contact him.

"Under normal conditions you would not be sent so soon after taking the habit but we've had applications in with this school—surely the most prestigious in the country—for years, and this opening is too good to pass up. They have had a late cancellation that is providential for us.

"Years ago when we launched our plans for birthing centers we had an influx of registered nurses avid for a contemplative life in tandem with the profession of midwifery. We were complimented that so many were accepted at the big university systems," she hunches her shoulders as if conserving warmth, her voice deepens, "little did we know . . . and thus, could not foresee the parabola of conflict that would bisect their experience.

"I have a dream that somewhere the old wisdom is being taught. Saddleback has the reputation of being different, founded by midwives . . . run by midwives . . . well, enough of that. I haven't told them you are a religious, labels, labels, never liked labels, God and you know who you are.

"I've told them you have been living in our extern quarters—that will explain some of the dates on your curriculum vitae—and have quite good experience in health care. They have a room for you. Your fees have been paid, and the sisters have voted you the use of the Ford Pinto for a year; oh, yes, and a small stipend. You haven't said a word."

"Too relieved."

"You thought the plan would be vetoed?" I nodded. "You have a good mind, Sister Mark, and you have heart. When you bring intellect and heart to the rising Spirit you'll be something," there is a splash of fireworks in her eyes. "Or nothing." She grins. "You had better get some sleep. You can pack your few things in the morning, it's a goodly drive into the wilds of Kentucky."

Her voice stops me at the door, "Sister, try to keep your journal? I realize you're going to be very busy with the studies and all . . . but see what you can do."

CHAPTER 2

"**Goin hiking, are ya? wooden go hiking** if I war ya, lone woman goin hiking in them thar hill nod gud idii." He leans forward questioning the three old men to his right, "no sireee, nod gud idii, is it?" Dominos falling, heads shake. Rearranging the plug of tobacco, giving some not very favorable thought from his expression to its taste, he turns to his left, "wha ya think?"

A grizzled frail hand lifts, a blackened pipe is removed with care from a stained mouth, we wait as bleary eyes stare the question deep into the tobacco spattered earth. The head shakes solemnly from side. The pipe stem is reinserted. "Thar! see!"

"I wasn't going hiking."

He eyes me up and down, "Well, thas gud."

"That'll be elevenfifty," the young boy putting his hand out for the gas money pats his cap, then hooks his thumb around his belt buckle while his thighs and knees do that little balloon and swivel thing that men do who have been riding or thinking about it.

I smile at him, lift a hand in farewell to the five holding up the wall of the combination gas/grocery and get back into the Pinto. The Smoky Mountains are behind me, I'm in the Alleghenys now, the Appalachian Trail must cross somewhere near here.

I've left the tourist towns and the road has become a narrow, twisty crazed thing that I share with huge trucks that thunder down on me from nowhere; wheeling out from hidden side-cuts they slosh coal.

Humongous bites have been taken from the hills. Gaia . . . I avert my eyes from our shame. Without leaves, the gouges in her accordion-pleated topography are only too apparent.

CLOSED. A sign on the mile-high screen declares the Titanic has been shut down. I drive through the town of Relief, home of Saddleback School of Midwifery, and do not realize it until a shingle at the side of the road reads, TWO WINKS pop. 230. I have passed it. Retracing my path I notice the bleached sign that I missed, RELIEF pop. 500, and there on the hill, the new hospital.

The lobby is dark and deserted. I stand, enjoying the feel of the ground and an erect back. I'm conscious of the iron band about my shoulders, the ache at the tip of my spine. Thank God I made it.

A young woman is reading at the desk marked INFORMATION. I walk up to her and ask directions. Her eye continues along the line of text in the glossy; without breaking her concentration she reaches behind, a thin sharp sound ricochets off the polished walls as an envelope slaps down on the vinyl.

What did I expect? a ten piece band playing Dixie? I stand like a dolt. Finally, she looks up, puzzled. I seem to have lost my voice. "Up the hill, up the hill . . . the dorms are up the hill," her face turns back to her reading as the thumb jerks across the shoulder.

I back up, glancing at the blank face of the envelope with the Saddleback Crest. It seems to say any old hill will do, there are a lot around, take any old way. I am aware of a soft hand on my arm, "Come, my name is Mary, I'm an aide in the emergency, I'll show you the best way." Blessings on those warm brown eyes!

The road is incredible. If Mary hadn't told me this was the way I would never have dared to come. Narrow, collapsed in spots, it winds upward at an incline that would discourage anything but goats or mules, around doctor's quarters, staff quarters, barn, odd houses, chapel, old hospital, dorms; clinging where a

New Yorker would not believe anything could cling, precarious hospital hill.

And this is Wednesday Cottage, the original midwives' residence. The macadam drops off into the gorge from here. "Someone always gets it," the senior student watches my disbelief when she shows me the six-by-ten paper-thin addition to the living room that is my "room." The bed lies side by side with the common TV, separated by the slimmest of partitions.

"I will be fine," I say, lecturing myself silently for a lack of poverty of spirit.

Two a.m., the sagging cot, squealing and clanking, is the only sound in the settled house. Blessed quiet. I didn't see anything in town that could possibly distract from concentration and study. All traffic stops after dark and stars are bright in the night sky. A whiff of wood smoke comes through the window.

A deep, low rumble—not the wooden sound of monastery castanets—wakes me before dawn. How does a contemplative begin her day? On her back, on her knees . . . it makes little difference. Caught in that formless place between sleep and waking, I search the light. There is a crash. Someone pounds down the stairs. The bathroom door slams and my door jiggles in response. Feet trod heavily into the kitchen, a pot bangs. After five minutes of relative quiet, someone bolts out the back door. Footsteps hurry beneath my window on downhill.

I must see this place! Tomorrow, I'll be a contemplative. Hiking shoes, I pull a sturdy pair of shoes from a carton, pull on clothes and five minutes later am standing in the grey dawn. The right tire of the monastery Ford abuts an upended six foot slab of macadam. The alternate road, pulled by gravity, washed by water, went with the flow. I lean over the confusion of blacktop platters, staggering like modern megaliths toward the hospital, away at the end of the tumbled road the roof is visible.

Turning, I look upward. High over the cottage, a grey stone castle sits on a battlement, a whiff of an Arthurian legend brightening in the rising sun. Hundreds of spiky green clumps dot the hillside. Climbing, I break chives off, nibbling, leaning hard into the hill. Past the old hospital which, made of chunky blocks of grey, was designed not to slide down hill.

I'm breathing heavy when I get to the chapel. Dankness and darkness hit me as I open the door. Stained glass windows facing East are just beginning to color. No light hits the altar or the dark wooden pews. I could make my morning prayer here, but I don't feel like staying. Digging around the edges of two round boulders embedded in the hillside, I roll them to the threshold, lift them, and prop open the door. This makes me feel good, I start running. At the summit, the sun shines on the hill behind the hill behind the hill. A rooster crows.

The rumble of coal trucks starts before dawn, like a heart beginning to thrum, like a ritual. As they wind through the town's thirty odd buildings it sounds like the National Guard is out.

This morning as Judy—one of the sophomores—and I talk, a roar of energy and noise approaches the kitchen door; the screen is jerked outward, the inner door thrown open, and there is Bobbi. We ate at the same table last night and I got an unfamiliar case of indigestion. Ellen, as usual, is right behind her. The two women collide, the first stopping abruptly when she sees me.

The wide, tight stance, hands on hips, the bark: "Well! wajado today?" She has barked this every day, twice a day, for the past three; I begin to feel some salvation of hers rests on my answer. I want to take this young woman by the shoulders and tell her that somehow, everything is going to be OK. Buffeted by the tense stridency within her, I smile and nod.

Bobbi and Ellen are classmates. One is never still, one is a pool of sadness, continually rubbing a pained, lower back. Whenever a noise in the living room indicates a presence, she appears at the heater in the main flow of traffic and starts rocking.

It's like something out of Mother Goose and Grimm: I play the dialogue in my head . . . do you have a license to do that? you need a license, if you're not a rock musician. What? a license? Since when does a body need a license when she has a pool of sadness sooo deep?

If Ellen isn't at the heater, Beatrice bursts out of the room next to mine. Planting herself before me in the hall she asks, "How goes things?" I haven't yet made the right answer, she goes languidly on her way muttering, "We'll wait and see." She has a friend staying with her; it's kind of neat, running into a male on the way to the bathroom.

I feel like a visitor from outer space. Most of the talk is about the tortures that await us. There is so much pent up emotion here it's a wonder the house hasn't slid downhill.

On the fourth day, waking to the rumble, feeling it

reverberate off the hills and through the timbers of the house, the fire, banked since investment, flares like a bunsen burner wide open on oxygen.

Doors close above me. The toilet flushes. Feet pound. Two people start a loud irritated conversation in the kitchen. I lie on the flimsy cot and burn. The deep layers . . . the radiant . . . the light, free momentarily from the bondage of matter and sense, timeless, for this I live.

Ever needful of fixing material form after these episodes I scramble about in the kitchen looking for ingredients for muffins. In the next hour, seven women stop to pass the time of day. Not communicate, pass the time. I register violent perturbation of mind, something being forced asunder.

"What are you doing here?" There are four women crowded in around me as I lift the last dozen muffins from the oven. The tall thin senior I know only as Linda repeats her question, "what are you doing here?"

"What do you mean?"

"You're a Nurse Practitioner."

I hadn't told anybody that but it is on my resume. I laugh, "our local paper calls them Supernurses." Four pair of eyes watch me. "I needed more knowledge of birthing. It's a welcome opportunity for in-depth study."

"Hah! Will we remind you of that!" Angry, disbelieving looks all around, "in depth!"

Linda plants herself directly in front of me, "Have you done any births?"

"Yes," and before she has the chance to ask more, "Aha! those muffins, two for my pocket and I'm off for a walk!"

A noisy, cheerful mob moves to engulf Lisa, a rangy blond woman with a warm, wide smile and the look of a colt that has just run the Preakness. The fifth of my class to arrive today she is assigned to the empty at the end of the living room. A fixed, brave smile does not hide the tightness around her eyes. When she can extract herself, she comes to my end of the table, "Did you go through that?!"

"Four days of it, glad you're here!"

After hours of joining-in I am suddenly very homesick and retreat to my cubicle. I sit on the narrow chair, feeling the noise on the other side of the flimsy wall and wonder if I should go for a walk. I've done a lot of walking. There are no lights on the road up past the hospital. There are wild packs of dogs. I could sit in the chapel, but it is an extremely cold, stone building. Anyway, I'm tired. I need refurbishing.

How can you concentrate with all this noise? a little voice within, asks. I can't. How can you sleep? I can't. The longing for the monastery is a palpable knot in my chest. Matins and Lauds would have been sung. The community has queued to bed, the monastery settled into a profound stillness, the red vigil light flickering in the chapel.

"There's only one way to treat that," sounds of TV and women talking come clearly through the wall, "you know what Doctor Douglas says."

"When they started the IV the arm blew up like a balloon! I watched in shock, absolute shock! I told Doctor Roberts, I didn't think the needle was in the vein.

"'What do you mean it's not in the vein, I put it in the vein. God, nurse, why didn't you tie the arm down? God! why didn't you stop the IV?'"

"His lectures are OK. He jokes a lot; he's used to much bigger hospitals, I bet he's a good administrator.

"But you gotta do it, don't ask them, they can't make decisions at that point. You confuse them with too much information. Some of them even say that, 'Don't tell me about it, do it!'

"He laid us out in holy lavender, but I don't blame him. I mean, the place was totally disorganized, Morley must be going through menopause. Well, he really told her. Should see how smooth things are running now."

"The SGOT was high but no one would listen to me, I wanted them to put her on ISO from the start. When the CEPH FLOC and THYMOL came in you should have seen them scurrying to move her into the empty."

"Make sure he's closed his eyes, you can't test for tactile if he's peeking."

"Those cysts often turn malignant, that's the way it is. Rogers recommends x-ray q 3 years after 35."

"Isn't that a lot of mammogram?"

"Very little radiation with the newer equipment, gotta be safe."

"Fever . . . leukocytes in the spinal fluid . . . "

Like a pure, deep spring the thought surfaces, find space somewhere! Find a room of your own! One of my nieces sings a ditty about a purple pea in a green pea pod. Humming this I fall asleep.

CHAPTER 3

"**Y**ou wanna take a walk with your friends, He's butchering a hog," Mary nods, a smile of complicity on her good-natured face. "I'll keep my ears open about the apartment," her hand touches mine lightly as she disappears through the swinging doors to the ER.

Was it David Hume who said that things and self were only bundles of relations, nothing in themselves, nothing at all? I take one last look at the bulletin board; I've jotted down two addresses, bypassing the senior's note who has a small child and wants someone to share rent and child care.

"Mary's husband, He, is butchering a hog today, we're invited!" The announcement I deliver after three hours of sitting listening to an expert on local fauna, is greeted with whoops and hollers.

After lunch, five of us climb the

North-South ridge that throws the cottage in early afternoon shade. At the top we start gaily North.

We stop almost immediately. At the side of the trail, surrounded by a hedge gone to bramble, eight crumbling headstones poke out of the fallen leaves among faded, plastic flowers.

"It's the slave cemetery."

"What slaves?"

"They were buried here. It hung on, you know, a long time around here."

There is a long silence. "How do you know?"

"My folks are from here, of course there's no prejudice now."

"Now that I think of it . . . I haven't seen any black people."

"Well . . . they don't choose to live here, there aren't any within thirty miles."

Suddenly I feel as raw and abandoned as the cemetery . . . and tragically white. Compliments of Zora Neal Hurston.

Ester, sensing the gloom, starts marching, "left,

right, left, right." I ask Lisa what she's discovered in town.

"Nice little bookstore run by a retired midwife, with almost two hundred volumes on Appalachia. And a hardware."

"Not LA, is it?" We laugh.

"Teressa, here it is, this is it, isn't it?" We cluster about at the top of the ridge, looking down into the sun-drenched valley. Smoke drifts upward from the chimney of a rambling frame house. A Rhode Island red cackles and flaps her way around the corner of a shed, a determined rooster fast on her tail. "What's the best way down?"

Looking at each other we shrug. Hooting and hollering like banshees we slide. I am vaguely aware of people hurrying from the house, a woman laughing in deep, rolling sounds. There are leaves in my shirt, leaves in my hair, Ester has a leaf sticking out of her glasses like a flag.

"He is the only name he ever had," Mary says laconically as she leaves us to help him lift the hog with block and tackle. Once the hog is fastened, she glances at us sitting in the semicircle and then back at her husband; wiping her hands on her apron she turns and walks back into the house.

Before I realize He has the knife in his hand he has slit the five foot carcass open from stem to stern in one simple almost off-handed motion. Steam pours from the cavity, Anatomy 101 on hog has begun.

He identifies the spleen, the liver, the stomach; without a wasted motion, he makes two deft cuts, scoops the huge mass of pulsing blue into his arms, and then into a tub.

The man working rhythmically, the chicken sounds, the wood smoke, the sun . . . the light rises from my pelvis like a burnished apple.

"Drop the ears off fer ya." When we do not respond he continues, "give 'em ta the school every year."

"What for?" the response is unanimous.

"Yer suturing class," he looks at us as if we don't have the brains to be midwives.

The sheriff talks to us for two hours. He leans back in his chair, rests his hands on a mound of belly and tells us he has our own best interests at heart. His tone is fatherly.

"Guyni bars haven't been closed all that long. You feminists should be warned that stuff never took around here. Respect, that's what it's all about. Careful what you wear, don't go looking fer trouble, you'll be fine. People want to respect you, you behave right 'n' they will; you respect yourself and we respect you."

The local historian talks to us for three hours. The culture is rich, he says, it has probably been studied more than any other indigenous group in the United States. He gives us a list of books that can be obtained in town, tells us to check out the library. Take the opportunity now, he says, you will never regret it.

The town undertaker talks to us for two hours, then takes us through his embalming room. I would go anywhere at that point just to be able to stand and walk instead of sit. He tells us about how his family became undertakers here in Relief. How he became an undertaker. Different size funerals. The cost of caskets. The need for grief and his ability to provide circumstances for the surfacing of this very necessary grief. How people feel about death. How he feels—having graduated from college—about death.

"Feel it, go ahead feel it!" We are inspecting casket depths and padding, comparing the $500, $800 and $1,000 stuffing. My mind wanders back to the day I took the habit and the ornateness of the customary stark cell. When I first heard about the congregation that was involved in birthing and contemplation, how excited I had become. That someone there would understand about the inner light . . . this drew me.

So here I am, the burgeoning mystic and uncertified midwife, part of a group filing from a mortuary display room. Patience was never one of my strengths.

A middle-aged friendly woman, Mrs. Tandera Kane, is our only instructor, but a second has been hired and will arrive next month. The director of the school has been here three months. The director of the hospital has been here for a month and a half.

I have had two dead-ends house hunting. It is at least 1 a.m. before 'Wen' quiets down. I had forgotten how ridiculous TV fare can be. Since He slaughtered the hog, the light has not risen up my spine, the gold cobra has not turned over in her sleep.

I am sitting in an outpost clinic talking to a resident midwife/nurse practitioner. We have spent an hour discussing various aspects of birthing when she says, "Are you really sure you want this program?"

"I'm here," I don't know what else to say.

"You haven't seen anything yet, it gets much worse. They'll not help you, you know."

"I don't think I understand."

She looks very sad, "you'll be completely on your own, you'll be your own lifeline and support . . . You don't know!"

Today I saw quality. A handful of retired midwives pulled back to tell us of the beginnings of the service. We are rapt. Stories of mules, impossible slopes, spring floods, milking cows that kick, jeeps that get stuck, being shot at; "We needed a strong sense of humor and strong hands." "Things were different." Each outpost had a nurse, a midwife and a cow.

"Things were different." One tinges the phrase with regret, another, sadness, a third is resigned, she speaks of change as impossible to stop.

The last to speak is a midwife/doctor who perches on the counter top like a tiny brown wren. She talks about the changes that have taken place in birthing practice. When she says she will not be teaching this year I feel sadness.

"You see what we tried to do! don't you?" she says suddenly. Starting at the other end of the room her gaze swings over the group. One by one they look down. When her eyes meet mine I can no longer stand the lack of spoken response, "yes!" I say.

"Have you done any births?"

"Yes."

She nods, as if that says it all, and sighs. She looks for one moment as if she is going to cry, then, shakes her head, hops down from the counter, "Well . . . if there aren't any questions, I wish you luck, I certainly do!"

Today we hear about snake handlers from a hospital administrator. He tells us about the practices of a dozen local churches, "writhing and stomping and yelling" and the attitudes on women that "held on around here." Morals and personal lives are important if we expect to be accepted and do our job well . . . and hair, too much of it on our heads is not acceptable. Unshaven legs—not acceptable. "Not a one of us would jeopardize our ability to do a service by our appearance now, would we?"

Bagels and lox! I just happen to be sitting next to him at the long table. I can just imagine the body language as I try to lean far from the man's field without seeming too obvious. When he offers us a ten minute break after an hour and a half, I bolt from the room.

"Is anyone bothered by this preparation of an elite for service?" Veronica, Ann and Becky look at me blankly.

Becky shakes her head and laughs. "Oh Teressa, you're too much! We're just bored out of our trees, that's all."

Muttering to myself, I drift down the corridor to the ladies room. It must be me, the problem in my head. Yet, I remember an admonishment of Simone Weil's about the admixture of good and evil being the greatest evil; it was our duty to make the distinction, she said.

Midway down the hall a woman from housekeeping is sweeping. She stops and watches me. Even with her, I nod, "good afternoon."

"Mary seys ye be lookin fer an apartmen," she speaks in a reedy voice.

Excitement flares. "Yes! Yes, I am."
"I know a woman up "owl" has a place."
"'Owl'? Is it difficult to find?"
"I kin draw ye a map."

We have an hour an a half longer with this man. I cannot bear to sit in the vicinity of his vibes for one more additional moment, I go to the very end of the conference table to an empty chair.

He's late. When he arrives all twelve of us have gathered and are sitting quietly. He glances at the now empty chair on his left. "Where'd she go?"

Ester giggles under her breath. Eleven heads turn as one to where I sit. "Oh, she moved down there." I don't look up, I sit in a glow looking at the rough map in my hands.

CHAPTER 4

Saturday morning the giant wash on the north of town is busy digesting the week's grime. Behind the Pinto, a monster of a truck pulls out of traffic; heading toward the stalls he stops with a crunch of brakes, inches from the monster in the bay. The driver climbs up on his cab, there is a lot of yelling and good natured waving as he tries to hurry things along. He gets hosed. Swinging like a chimp back inside he revs the motor and begins to push, there is a crunch of metal.

The man in the bay hosing down his truck looks startled and leaps for his door. We make room for him as he eases out into the line of traffic, scattering skeeter-plats of soap. Coal trucks come by in the opposite lane, the drivers grinning down on the wee pickups.

The drivers stop to talk. All traffic stops; those nearest frankly listen, no one puts a finger to a horn.

As I cross the East fork of the river all coal traffic drops away. The map waves gaily from my hand above the wheel. Climbing up from the river, three hundred feet above water level there is a car lodged in a tree. Only then do I notice other signs of flooding: odd scraps of lumber, doors, windows, there is even half a porch sitting all by its lonesome.

The road narrows and there is only enough room for one car. It weaves behind an excavated hill, a gravel pit, into a secluded hollow. For two miles a dozen frame houses straggle along the road, like deserted summer camps, then all sounds of traffic fade.

The road has left the little settlement and is cutting across a frozen bog. Cattails are making squeegee sounds against the windows when I hear the other car. I stop, flustered, I will have to back all the way to the last of those houses. But the oncoming driver acts fast. He bounces up the rise, sees me, reverses, all in one motion. Revving the engine of the truck, he disappears the way he came, pulling off rapidly, flattening the cattails in a wave.

I roll my window down as I pass him to thank him. He tips his hat and smiles. I leave the window down from then on, pulling another sense to my aid. Busy watching the sides of the road for possible turnoffs I come up to the foot of the mountain. The road ahead gives me heart chill. It goes straight up. A thousand feet above the valley floor it angles abruptly left.

Putting the Ford in low, taking a deep breath, I start. Nothing good happens after the steep climb and the abrupt turn. The road narrows. A space has been cut out of the mountain for three quarters of a car and immediately after this "rest" it narrows again and climbs. Another mile, everything opens out and I have driven into the black maw of an abandoned mine. Hissing and spitting, vents all along the shale release steam into the cold morning air. The yawning black hole gapes at me, this is not a place I would choose to stop.

I back up and look at the map Iah gave me. The road does not end here, there is a clearing ahead that looks like a river channel during dry season. That must be the "road." And this turnoff, half a mile up the river bed, this is exactly where it should be; I see why they call it "owl's nest."

"Thrudum . . . thrudum" . . . the swollen base sound hits my ears as I pull the car off into the scrub and drive the double rut around a bend. "Thrudum . . . thrudum . . ." a tiny man swings a rounded, long-handled maul. He doesn't look much taller than the tool.

Water laughs and gurgles over rock as I pull the Pinto off beside a shed opposite him. He rests his maul. His eyes are the color of a bluebird's tuxedo. Shifting the maul, he sticks out his hand and grins a great, wide toothless grin.

"Mighty fine bass," he says his eyes twinkling. I look at the tree raised on a couple of rollers. It sports two wedges, each driven about ten inches into the heart and as we watch a dark worm wiggles from the wedges and there is a low rasping sigh, "two more's all."

"Wedges?"

"Gluts." I never heard the word before and start to ask him about it but he takes my hand, "Cumin meet the missus."

If he is tiny, she is minute. In one smooth motion she clears everything from the double bed to the floor, gesturing for me to be seated. Then, hopping up beside me, "How lovely! it's so nice to have visitors. Do you believe in Jesus Christ?"

Before I leave Dan and Tempi and they direct me up the ruts to their daughter and son-in-law who have a cabin to let, I buy a pieced top for a future quilt, a lovely bright basket design of yellows. I tell myself the sisters can finish it and Reverend Mother can give it to some benefactor as a gift.

A lanky man ambles my way as I park the car half a mile up from their house. His eyes and hair are dark and bright as coal. When I have finished explaining why I have come he utters something between a yodel and whale song, a deep, warbling musical sound that is a pleasure to listen to, but tells me nothing for I don't understand a word.

"Would you spell it?" He yodels again. "Spell it?" I plead.

"H u r l." As if I am some engaging but stupid child he spells it out, laughter making his eyes shine. Then he gestures to the house.

To the sides of the stove a woman and four children sit watching me with wide, expectant eyes. "Vasti," he repeats it twice for me. A movement of her hand and the space on the couch widens for me. "Please sit," she says, smiling. Again I repeat why I have come. The man and woman talk back and forth in that yodeling song-like communication that leaves me baffled.

Hurl rises but I continue sitting. Vasti leans forward, "you better go with him."

At the door he turns, "Ya gotta man?" He enunciates clearly and I understand.

"Yes," I say after a brief hesitation.

"Children?"

"No."

He nods to the floor and walks out the door. I hurry to catch up with him. Past the immediate outbuildings I follow, deep on up into the hollow, across a footpath, over felled logs, around a wide area where someone has cut a dozen three inch saplings off twelve inches above the ground until, stopping at a clearing, he says, "thars one."

It's so dark I do not see the forest-green house until we are right on top of it and I know instantly that I cannot live in it. Three simple rooms are no problem, one could function as a kitchen, outfitted with appliances, there is a dry sink in one corner, the heat stove is in good condition and there is a porch. But it is much too dark, the scrub around the outside walls acting like shutters.

We look at another, a smaller version across the creek. Then, we walk back down toward his house, out of the darkness into the light. Breaking from the straightaway he heads up the hill. A rough hewn cabin sits on poles, "Thaw the oldest boy," he says, stepping back to let me enter.

A large black stove sits just inside the door. Rough hewn trees running along the ceiling span the width of the cabin and disappear out the far wall. There is a refrigerator in the second bright room opposite a large dry sink; a wide black hose attached to the sink drain drops through a hole in the floor away out onto the dirt. Light pours in the windows.

"Need a cook stove," he says. Turning, I follow him up the wide plank stairs to the second floor.

Impose the fewest number of conditions . . . She will respond out of her fullness! The loft is large and airy and bright. Three rough pillars hold up the roof. There are windows at the east and west.

"Thar's tha outhouse," he points out the west window up the hill.

I turn to him, "water?"

"Gud well."

"Electricity?"

"Company needs turn it on."

"How much would you ask for rent?"

He shrugs, purses his mouth, "Thirty-five. Leave ya to think it over," and with that he turns and clumps down the stairs. I stand and listen as his feet crunch the gravel between the houses.

Let's be calm now, I lecture myself. Look the situation over thoroughly, this isn't exactly camping out but it's no motel either. Go back, look at the other two. Out of the cabin, past the well, on up the hollow, I retrace my steps.

The first one we looked at is clean and seems new; the paint is unscratched, there is paneling in one room. No, it is much too dark.

Crossing the dry creek bed to the third cabin I notice holes. This house, far up the dark cleft of the hollow is surrounded by holes one to three feet deep. Someone has been digging for water?

I am straining to find the bottom of a hole under the darkness of the overhang. It is full of water and the reflection of the vines above duplicate the swirling patterns on the surface. When the eye surfaces, cold, unblinking mercuric eye staring up at me, my heart rises into my mouth. As my breath slows, it holds its position with the barest of undulations, twenty inches of brown lake trout, diameter of a circle she cannot widen, cannot bend.

A curious welter of emotions propels me back out of the hollow. They are keeping her fresh, I tell myself . . . yes, yes, of course, silly. Climbing back up to the cabin on poles I sit on the flat porch along the south wall dangling my legs. Jean Cocteau speaks about killing the critic within and being persuaded only by that which speaks violently to the sexuality of your soul. He was talking about art, but it always seemed to me that he was talking about life. This is it, the thing that calls forth a spontaneous inner erection. This cabin has been waiting for me.

When I return to Wednesday Cottage Lisa and Ester are footloose in the kitchen. "You found a place! We've got to see it!"

"Now?!"

Back we drive up over that mountain. It is worth it, their enthusiasm is so overwhelming it washes away my remaining doubts. Upon returning to hospital hill they tell the world, but there is no joy.

It is nine thirty, the radio is picking up Brahms, the classical station in Cincinnati fading in and out. Heavy footsteps enter the living room and cross to my door. There is a loud knock.

"Heard yer movin." Two senior students I do not know stand in my doorway; I don't invite them in, there isn't any room.

"Yes, I found a place," I smile, "it doesn't have a lot of amenities, but . . ."

The shorter woman cuts me off, "You movin because you don't like us?" She stares.

How do I answer? I am embarrassed for her. Trying to hide this as best I can, I smile, tell her I am older, need space and quiet for study. Their eyes are watchful, they wait. There must be something I haven't said, what is it I wonder, what will get rid of them? I mention the lack of running water and the fact that I'll probably be longing for a hot tub bath.

"Well," the shorter of the two says, "you can always come back."

The tall woman intersperses this with, "You'll be moving back, you know. There is no way you'll have time. Your studies will suffer."

After the delegation leaves and climbs the stairs to

their classmates on the cottage's second floor, I shut the door and sit and pour myself an inch of wine. Just to wash the taste out of my mouth. Separateness is evidently their sin. They do not know yet that separateness, physical separateness from others, is going to become increasingly inconsequential. Separateness from the inner core of your being, that's sin!

"We're the last class, school's closing."
"That's what I hear too, there are hardly any teachers left." Twelve women from ten different states, we have been remarking on the turmoil we are finding. "It's all very hush-hush someone says, but four out of six midwives resigned this fall. They sent out a call to the alumni to come and teach for a year." "God, we're lucky we got in!" "I slept in my car when I came for the interview." "I slept up in the chapel on one of the benches." "Wasn't it hard?" "Do you know fifty were turned down for the last class?" Half a dozen came anyway, they're working in the hospital, taking the physiology course, and hoping to get in next year.

We are meshing into some resemblance of family. Shared laughter, submerged groans, looks of disbelief when our instructor Mrs. Kane tells us we are to have a three hour class this morning with a man from the Bureau of Mines.

But first, our orientation to the hospital library. A self-assured young man smoothes his hair, pokes a comb back in his hip pocket, and defines "reference material"; we watch absorbed as the zipper on his "fly" steals silently down.

His laconic presentation on the arrangements of the texts which somehow become un-arranged, the placements of the periodicals, which we have if someone gives them to us and no one takes them away, and the green box over there, with the stuff you'll need that I don't know anything about, has me bursting a gut on violently suppressed laughter.

As soon as he leaves the room I turn to Lisa with the weight of it. She was looking around for the green box and when she realizes he meant the file cabinet, something resembling a neigh begins deep within her. In thirty seconds tears are running down her cheeks.

"Was anyone else watching his zipper?" Diane asks. We howl.

Allison stands and wrings her hands if she cannot sit in the chair by the window. Ester has been running for it and plopping herself down just to observe the reaction. But she has stopped, it is obvious Allison is in distress. Lisa throws herself from the metal chair to the floor every now and then, her expression wry. She has had it.

"You play, 'here's the church, here's the steeple . . . where are the people?' when you violently disagree, Tess," Ann says, giggling in amusement.

Beverly doesn't say a word for days on end. Then, as if starved for cogent discourse, launches into a soliloquy. Very rational, very precise, she will explain what has just been touched on in class in great depth, then, shut up for three more days.

We are in our early twenties to late thirties and seem to be divided into three semi-distinct groups. The very young, who haven't done much nursing and who figure midwifery is as good as other branches and may be cleaner and more autonomous. The older ones, who have come far enough in the profession to know it is no longer an option—nursing—but who need to support themselves— this is their OK Corral.

Then there is the motley middle group. Here, I clump those who idealize the situation, and those who intellectualize the situation. Some of these women feel that birthing practice in the States is in deep trouble. Some want to climb administrative ladders and do something about it. Some simply want to infiltrate the system. I put myself in this group the first time I responded to a woman and her husband who wanted a home delivery. We are family.

CHAPTER 5

As clouds slide silently down hill and moil in the valley I skip orientation to the town library to buy myself a broom. I am a woman with space of her own, a loaf of bread, four bananas and a broom, happily exiting the Thriftway when a nappy head plows into me.

I respond too slowly. I see the determined little figure, eyes pursed in the fixing of her thought, arms working like pinions to push the world behind her. Four foot eight, maybe eight or nine years old . . . she steams my way, but all I do is stand there.

Large brown eyes in a slender face look up in surprise, "Please excuse me, ma'am." I am thinking she really must be older than I had guessed, she speaks so correctly, so politely. "I'm going to have breast of chicken."

"Well, that sounds good." I stop inanely, watching her nod the delicate oval chin in determined agreement. It is very much in her mind, this chicken. "Be careful of these doors though, this one is supposed to be for people leaving the store, that one there is for going in. They hit when you're not looking."

She is taking this elementary information in matter-of-fact like, when a woman's brown hand is placed on her shoulder. "Burnet, doan you run from yer mamma like that! Girl, you hear?" The woman tips the child's chin up firmly with her other hand. Rebelliousness flairs on the small face, but the determination on the mother's seems to cool her youthful ardor. She looks down, then, turning with great deliberation, walks back toward the cars.

"I should have named her Ergot, she's too damn full of herself for the modest Saxifrage," she watches the girl's back in grudging admiration. "But, I fell in love with the the Scarlet Pimpernel. The woman's broad black face crinkles up in an infectious, exasperated grin. She looks to be in her middle thirties. A black woman dressed in a long denim skirt, boots, heavy bulky sweater, wearing a chatreuse/green turban around her head and gold hoops in her ears. I feel like I'm back in New York.

She turns to me now. The young girl is lighter in color, her face oval, while the older woman's is square—I think of Meso-American. But the mother-daughter connection is definitely seen around the eyes. The older dark eyes are now looking at me with decided interest. "Thank you fer seeing she didn't bang her head."

"She's lovely . . . a very determined young lady!"

"You're new around here. At the hospital?" I nod. "Humm . . ." She pulls herself up, frowns a little, seems about to say something and thinks better of it. The look she gives me is searching.

"Well," I say, gesturing with the broom in one hand, package in the other . . .

"My name is Seuell Connor," her hand starts my way, then realizes mine are engaged. "Well, maybe we'll see each other around."

"Mine is Teressa Mark."

Three carloads of junk later, three trips down the mountain, I survey my swept floors by the light of my flash. I wish I could stay, but I don't have a bed.

The sinuous column of joy that prefers the spinal cord, climbs like a child on a jungle gym. Hand over hand, feet up, roll, gain momentum . . . go for the next bar . . . roll. After some little infinity I leave and walk down to the car. Dan and Tempi's gate light goes out in my rear view mirror as I turn from the ruts onto the boulder-way of "owl."

This morning, the Bureau of Social Services, the theme: The Meshing of Systems in Health Care. This afternoon, the Department of Education's representative tells us the school system is looking forward to our individual presentations. We look dumb. "Oh yes, I haven't told you yet, but each of you is required to present something in the local schools," Mrs. Kane says with forced nonchalance.

After class I do not loiter for one moment but climb hospital hill to Wednesday Cottage, gather cleaning materials, pail, mop, jump in the car and head out to "owl."

I am hanging a small Buddhist wind chime under the eave by the door when Hurl walks over with Michael, aged three. He smiles, nods, but doesn't really look at me. He holds Michael up to feel the slender brass rods. We sit on the porch in the afternoon sun. Two kittens materialize and throw themselves on Michael who rolls back on the planks, laughing, the weight of them on his chest.

The sun, the chimes, kittens and child rolling and laughing . . . we don't search each others eyes, we barely look at each other this man and I. And we don't speak. We "set awhile" and when he gets up to leave I trust him more than anyone else in the county. As they walk back to their house followed by the two frisky kittens, I start hauling buckets of cold water from the well to the coal-blackened interior of the cabin.

"Forty goat and fourteen kid." Dan is gesturing at the roof of the barn barely visible in the hollow below, "was plenty o room fer the goat, it was the kid that did it, we moved up here cus of the kid. I'm 82, you know," he grins his wide grin.

We have been discussing where to buy lime for the outhouse, the least expensive food stores, kindling, wood. "Say hello?" he takes my answer for granted; Tempi will have put her teeth in, she waits at the door, wearing a flowered apron two sizes too big.

"I don't do as much as I used to but I kin teach," she says, nodding at the smallest of the three frames, "thas a beauty now, isn it?"

"Ya need a char?" Dan points to whorls of bark drying in the head space above the stove.

"I do," . . . I am suddenly aware of the fact that I have no furniture at all. "I need to find a couple of planks and two crates for a desk . . . and yes, I do need a chair."

"I make ye a char, Hur loan ye a desk."

"How much would you charge me for the chair?" I am vividly aware of what I will save by renting the cabin as the dormitory fee is high. But I am also painfully aware of how quickly money goes, dribbling away. "OK."

He drifts around behind as I bend to check Tempi's draw stitch on the small quilt, and I know my seat is being measured for the "char."

We have been assigned to obstetrics for the day. As we undress and hunt about through the hamper of tossed and unmarked scrub gowns, a tall young woman with blond hair watches from her position by the open door. As the gown falls over my head, the door sighs closed. "Didn't think I'd have to be strip searched to get on the ward. Who was that!?"

"She's a senior, has a little girl," Beverly's grin is rueful as she tightens the drawstring at her waist.

"Couldn't find my pantyhose," I exclaim, "we've heard so much about the unprofessionality of hair . . ."

"Ah, it won't matter," Bev says throwing up her hands and leaving the locker room.

Sitting in the nurses' station listening to report, I glance from my unshaven legs to the sleek stocking legs of the seniors. Feeling like a wart hog I stretch another inch from the much washed cotton at my knee.

"Sorry there aren't more patients," the senior student says, finishing report. "You'll get your twenty births, either at Ludwig or Raybird County."

Mention of the twenty births necessary for certified nurse midwifery status, and the fact that most of our experience will be obtained in big city hospitals, pulls me up short.

The senior who eyed us while we undressed waits for me, her name is R. B., I am to follow her on rounds. In the first room a young woman in a pink negligee drops the push button phone with a "gotta go, midwife's here." "How are we today?" the senior directs me with a nod of her head to pull the curtains. There is discreet laughter. R. B. checks the breast binder and then the peri-pad for lochea. She says a few words to the young girl. Everything slows to professional time. I curtail my movements, instinctively fixing a bland face.

The young girl recites a litany on the care of the newborn. "Ah! very good!" says R. B.

"I hope I haven't caused too much trouble!"

"You've been an excellent patient"

"I try to follow orders, I was just telling my friend on the phone there it's a real lucky thing I had a midwife that knew what she was doing," she laughs. "I'm OK then?" she looks back and forth between the two of us.

"You're fine! . . . you're just fine. But you've got to keep doing those exercises I told you about."

Noncommittal student-smile on my face, I follow R. B. into the second room. A woman bending over a rounded bundle in the center of the bed, pulls erect; withdrawing a finger from a tiny clenched fist, she nods distractedly, her attention is clearly elsewhere.

"I'm so sorry, I couldn't help it." She holds up the tiny infant bottle, "he was so hungry!" The baby is put back in the bassinet while binders and pads are checked. R. B. says "tch, tch." The specter of fat unhealthy babies, who grow to fat unhealthy children, who grow to fat unhealthy adults is wheeled out in all its misery, replete with statistics on disease. The lines across the woman's forehead deepen. She says, "I'm sorry!" When she says it for the third time, I turn and leave.

When R. B. comes from the patient's room she eyes me for a moment with her head to one side as if she's going to speak. Then, "There's no one in delivery, but we have a woman in early labor."

"Rosanna, how are you doing?" The dark woman lying on the stretcher with the IV running in her arm looks our way. Labor is all hard edges and very clean, a most modern surgical suite. "They're getting stronger," the woman's eyes are apprehensive.

"That's good! that's good! we're going to keep close eyes on you now," R. B. checks the intravenous and pats her hand. Back in the corridor, "Well, have you any questions?"

"Do you start IV's on all laboring women?"

She nods. "Doctor's orders."

"Wouldn't it be better during the early stages of labor to be up and around? Especially with normal births. . . ?"

"We don't have any normal births here." That response stymies me. She sees my hesitation, "in the event medication is needed it's better to have the access route established." Her voice softens, "we don't have any normal births, every birth shows some abnormality. It is better to anticipate than to be sorry." She waits.

"What is this ceiling on feedings, who makes it?"

"What do you mean?" The dark eyes are annoyed.

"Who dictates how much the mothers can feed their babies?" There! that's clear enough.

She pulls herself up tall, this is evidently a touchy subject. "You better forget everything you've learned up 'til now, they do things differently here!" With that she strides into the nursery for the mandatory three-minute scrub.

We scrub side by side in silence. When she leaves I continue scrubbing, scrubbing, scrubbing.

A dapper, greying little man, Doctor D., appears to take report on the five babies. The air is thick with deference. He rapid-fires questions on newborn jaundice. He shoots Barbara, Ann and I a counterplot look as the senior students stumble; when the eldest takes charge and answers, in a voice that has nothing jovial about it, he barks, "You forgot!" . . . and reels off figures while the student blushes. "Next time be prepared!" he says.

The report ends with everyone on their toes. He smiles and nods. Bobbing like a bantam rooster, he turns to leave.

"We'd like to ask about the feedings." He rolls toward the sound of R. B.'s voice, rocks on the balls of his little feet, looks her over coolly. Then he turns to the rest of us, gauging the extent of the threat, "Is that one and a half ounces a BIG problem for you girls?" his eyes are challenging.

I hesitate, it is as if there is no one in the room but me and this little man who rolls on the polished floor as if his feet will not keep still.

"Yes," I say after a long moment, and beside me I hear the aide also say, "yes!" No one else opens her mouth. The eyes settled on my face then move down my body. For one long moment he stares at my legs. "Oh, why don't you make it two then," he says almost offhandedly. He has turned and is gone. He did not look at the aide.

"Good for you!" "Miserable ceiling!" "Should have changed it long ago!" "Two ounces makes more sense!" "See! we can change things." The incredible tension is gone.

At the end of the day on obstetrics I do not feel like eating, and drive out of town. Over the river, on up past the blacktop, Dan is working at the shave horse in the yard; he smiles and nods, but doesn't speak.

I squat, my back against the sideboards of the

house, listening to the whoosh . . . whoosh . . . whoosh of the draw knife. Sitting on a long bench, one foot holding a dumbhead vise against a log, he draws the knife down repeatedly, a proliferation of blond curls pile at his feet.

Water murmurs, chortles and sings behind us. There is a soft thud as he drops a finished leg. He picks up a new one; there is another thud as he discards it. Choosing another, he views it from all angles; satisfied, he fixes it in the vise, whoosh, whoosh, whoosh the pile grows.

There is no circulation in my feet when I stand, but the tension has eased from my neck and shoulders. I touch him lightly on the shoulder and leave. The hardware is open late tonight, I drive into town to buy three gallons of inexpensive white paint.

CHAPTER 6

"**I doan care ta.**"

"Oh, well . . . OK." Twenty minutes later, after much warning foot stomping on the porch, Hurl sticks his head back in the doorway. His hand is out.

"Here tis." I stop painting to look at the replacement light. "I thought you didn't care to?"

"Yup."

"I'm up a shuck trying to understand you."

"Up a shuck? Corn?" His bright coal eyes look to where I stand three rings up the ladder.

"Like, totally useless." I grin down at him. "Like, I haven't got a prayer of a chance . . ."

"Prayer of a chance . . . up a corn shuck, huh?"

"Yup."

"Like tha," he says, and doubles over with laughter, gasping "corn, corn, corn," while slapping his thighs.

The variant twang, the strange phrase . . . the rolling hills are on his tongue, "Noun locks doors," he says.
"You gotta be kidding!"
"Yagoddabekiddin . . . wha does tha mean?" Harlin asks, coming up behind us. I construct a verbal-hand-signal-facial-hash and end up with the tears running down my face. Invariably I ask him to spell it.
"John Harvey Washington!" Hurl's emphasis flattens the prevalent roll, "I tol ye he's jus doan the road."
"I been down the road. Guess I asked the wrong question. I had no luck whatsoever finding that used furniture store," I shrug my shoulders.
"Show'd a said ya was a nurse, next time say tha . . . doan forgit, they respec nurses," he walks off.

I am painting around the refrigerator when Ester, all rosy-cheeked and smiling peeks around the doorjamb. "I didn't hear a car!"

"Walked. Well, where do you want me to start? Gorgeous day out there. You said you'd welcome help."

I shake off my surprise, "how, how about the loft?"

Many crackers, sandwiches, cookies and beers later Hurl is back carrying a piece of furniture, "Loan ya a desk . . . where ya wan it?" When he returns from the loft he is shaking his head in amazement, "never look so gud! Ayahs thinkin abou changin tha ren," he nods at the floor while we wait, "twent-five's znuf," he nods decisively at the floor and walks out the door.

Soon after, waving away my offer of a lift back to the hospital, Ester goes striding off down the road. Quiet settles like a lovely down comforter. I close the plank door and climb the stairs to the loft. Although the sun is reaching the horizon, the house sits so high that light continues to pour into the loft, washing the newly painted walls rose. Sitting down on the bare fiberboard I face the sun, my back against the first pillar.

Anything of importance cannot help but be unrecognizable since it bears no resemblance to anything already known. I can no longer remember who said that . . . it bears no resemblance to anything already known . . . the words repeat themselves, insistent.

It is after ten when I loop the rawhide latch at "owl." Behind the swaying trees, Vasti and Hurl's Christmas lights flicker. The sky is brilliant with stars.

At the hospital, stopping to check my mail, I find a note from Reverend Mother wrapped around an airline ticket. Come home for Christmas! it says. What a lovely surprise! I must wrap up my preparations on the cabin then, have it all geared up and ready to go for that frenzy of class after the holidays.

There is no tub like an old tub! Paws, squat sturdy legs, high sides, non-existent overflow. The introduction to Tannhauser . . . its amphorical vortex accompanies me while I strip, pour beer, put it alongside lemon oil, scissors, soap, nail file, on the flat rim, and lower my begrimed body below the waters. Wednesday Cottage has one thing going for it—its tub.

I am a seal, blow holes barely out of water when the knob rattles on the bathroom door, "Who's in there?" The voice is muffled, "is Terry Mark in the tub again!"

"Yes, I'm in the tub," some of the warm water sloshes up my nose, I cough.

There is laughter in the living room, "You should have seen her when she came in."

"Don't tell me she's still working on that cabin! Where is this place anyway?"

"You mean she has to haul water and coal!?"

"It's a nice quiet spot," I recognize Lisa's alto.

"She's crazy! She'll never have time."

"She'll manage," the final comment is Ester's and with it the talk wanders off . . . " Guess who I saw walking up the hill from Sue Puffin's place before dawn Tuesday morning?"

"Duranski!"

"No, he's been replaced," the voice is smug.

Three names are mentioned and discarded. "Well! tell me then!"

"Morey!"

"No! That little shrimp!"

"He hasn't been sleeping in the dorm," the speaker ends on a high note that turns to laughter.

It is nine a.m. on a Tuesday. We are sitting around the omnipresent conference table watching the Director of Psychological Services play with the bowl of his unlit pipe; "Helps me think," he says. Greying receding hair, soup strainer mustache, he reminds me of a condensation of the late Carl Jung.

He has been talking about the numbing effect of strangeness, the perceptual eddy and the resulting disjunction; the inability to think clearly, the resulting anger. "It's a very normal thing in foreign surroundings," he peers over the rims of his glasses, adagio parentalis, "to be pierced by loneliness . . . depressed . . . and oftentimes, very angry. Once we have embraced uncertainty . . . " his voice drones on.

Once we have embraced uncertainty . . . the words fall like gold leaf. At the center of my pelvis, a nudge, then, a full fledged kick. Like a babe stretching in the belly, the sleeping one turns over. Not here, I think, O no, not here! She does not listen. Woken from the cave of her dreams by an essence, she rises, all of a piece.

"Miss Mark! . . . " the hard edge of a three-ringed binder hits me between the shoulder blades. Allison heads toward the door. "Miss Mark? you're the only one who hasn't scheduled an appointment."

"Sorry!" we are the only ones left sitting at the table, "I was lost in thought . . . "

"No matter. Now, when will it be convenient . . . " he turns the pages of his notebook.

After lunch I walk into the local hardware in search of stovepipe. There is no one in the outer room. I hesitate, then, hearing voices, stride through the doorway into the large inner packing room. Hurl has carted a newer version of a coal stove to my living room, rolling the other unceremoniously down the hill; I am exuberant and anxious to use the remainder of the afternoon to get my stove in order.

It is a big dark room, stacked to its high ceiling with crates, boxes, bales of wire, pipe and tools. Today it is full of men. Four of them, dressed similarly in dark blue shirts, work from a raised dias; ten or eleven customers mill around the floor, joking, calling out orders, trading quips with the clerks.

The cadaver, pulled from the morgue refrigerator on its metal slab, drops a cold hand on you; this is how silence falls. All eyes turn. It seems like an eternity, but finally a clerk shouts across in a gruff voice, "Yes?"

"I need to buy stovepipe."

He is curt, "You gotta wait." I nod.

I wait. And as I wait I curse myself for forgetting to fly my "be calm, I'm everyone's sister" signals. And I curse myself for forgetting to say I'm a nurse.

I wait as a man to my right smacks his lips.

I wait as another walks around behind, making the puckered sounds a trout makes scooping floating bait from the surface of a pond.

When an old bleary-eyed guy circles me twice, as if taking measurements, I move directly and purposefully to a corner of the raised dias where the clerks have resumed work in a subdued manner. A man drifts in front of me and simply stands and stares.

Within me there is a war going on. A war between the all-nurturing Mother who waits for them to grow up, and the great cat who waits no more but would chew them up and spit them out like a wasted wad. I stare him down. There is a spattering of chuckles as he drifts away. I need stovepipe. There isn't another hardware for thirty miles.

It is twenty minutes by their clock time when the young boy approaches me; the four clerks stand and watch. In a voice just beginning to deepen, "Ya wan'ed stove pipe . . . jus one section or two? I git it fer ya," he does not meet my eyes.

I have an old copy of *Country Woman* that shows you how to fit a damper in new pipe . . . I let the great cat chew into the blackened mess running through the ceiling of the cabin.

"Ye look so funny!" Vasti and the old coon dog have their heads cocked in opposite directions in the doorway.

"I did it!" I grin through soot-begrimed eyebrows and lashes.

"Never saw anythin like ye," she thrusts a grey battleship of a kettle forward and thinks better of it, "I better leave it here on the table . . . the stove they deliver work?" her large brown eyes dapple in the late afternoon light.

"All but two burners . . . that's why it was cheap, but I figure I don't need four burners."

"Ye git coal?"

"No." I take a deep breath, "I'm trying hard enough. Two people at the hospital said they would do the hauling, but nothing has happened," my voice trails off. "The thing is that I've been warned about getting it myself . . . they say I don't know anything about the grades, I'll end up paying far more than I should . . . I have to watch my money."

"It's cold! You take some of ours and fire up tha stove."

A half hour later, on my hands and knees mopping up the last of the black dust, I stretch to unhook the latch as someone stomps on the porch. Dan, grinning his tobacco-stained grin, hefts a delicate little chair with a woven seat and curved back, "Here's ya char."

"It's beautiful!" I get up off my knees, take the chair, which can't weigh five pounds, settle it on a level area by the stove, and sit. As I place my butt in the halfmoon seat, the bark settles, rustling. Four slightly curved legs give a little sigh. I grin. "I never had a chair made for me, it's cute as, cute as a bug's ear. You're good!"

He looks shyly downward, "made a lot of chars," he says while he tries to look nonchalant and the grin darts to his ears.

When I am pulling water to refill my jugs great feathery flakes begin to fall, I watch them compete with the smoke from my chimney. I am turning— water jugs in tow—to begin the climb when Hurl comes roaring up the hollow, squeals to a stop in the basketball court, reverses, revs the engine, and backs up past me to the empty coal hutch.

Immediately boys appear, shovels are handed around and everyone converges on the great mound of coal in the truck. I am afraid to believe and afraid to appear stupid. I mean, what claim have I, that this man should take an afternoon to haul coal for me? He definitely doesn't want to be bothered right now. At the moment I am in the way of some sort of male bonding activity. They laugh and avoid each others' shovels heaving-to the black mound. Up the path I go with the water jugs.

When I return Michael is hugging a chunk of coal to his chest. Staggering on stubby legs to the lowest wall of the hutch, with a mighty thrust and a loud grunt he heaves it over. I see they have thrown the larger chunks that will not fit in the shovels to one side, I join him in carrying them, both of us staying well out of the way of the shovels.

"Tha keep ya?"

"I don't know what to say."

"Drove creation 'n' back . . . cuddin fine wha I wanned . . . had ta go all tha way to . . . " he mentions an unfamiliar name.

"Hurl, I'm very grateful . . . " he waves it away. "Well . . . how much do I owe you?"

I have hung the last of the Georgia O'Keefe prints and am tacking to one side a little handwritten message she included in a letter to Sherwood Anderson in the 1920s: "Making your unknown known is the important thing." Hurl took $35 for the load of coal, nothing for the haul.

My hands, cracked in jagged seams between the fingers, are bleeding from too much cold water washing. I look at the pictures. Flashes of O'Keefe, fierce jack in the pulpit purples and greens, proudful, exclamatory, they spiral through the opening to the loft like Monet's dancers.

Vasti's grey tea kettle steams from its wrenched

spout. There are inexpensive but clean carpets on either side of the stove, a frayed blue linen cloth on the table. The cabin is ready. I have a bed, desk, chair and makeshift bookcase in the loft. A table, chair, rocker and a plank supported by two cinder blocks, comprise my living room furniture. The kitchen I've hung with plants and left empty, the refrigerator, cook stove, sink and shelving take up enough room.

Pouring a glass of wine, lighting a candle, I prop open the door. Night has fallen. The spit and fizzle of large flat pancakes of snow hitting the black belly of the coal stove is the only sound. A great sense of calm settles inside me.

There is a rustle, bump and bang as the muzzle of a coon dog appears at the knee of a boy of ten, a headless wonder, a haystack of kindling, his eyes arch over the top-most twig. "Let it fall," Vasti says. The boy watches in satisfaction as the whole tumbles noisily to the floor.

Vasti and I are down on our hands and knees when the kittens arrive. She finishes the last few sticks while I get milk and put the saucer out of way under the table. One kitten immediately begins to lap, the second, darting under the tail and belly of its brother approaches the milk under cover. When we look up for Harlin we are both silent. He stands midway up the steps to the loft, eyes as black as night, lost in the mythic colors and proportions of the O'Keefe prints.

CHAPTER 7

Will it always be more exhausting to get from Newark? Rigid, dipped in time warp, I watch as the taxi leaves monastery drive. Blinded silent windows face me, a red wall darkened by steady cold drizzle; the enclosure fence, starting at the edge of the old Edwardian mansion, surrounding the gardens and orchards, is blacker than black. The sign tessellates with cold, heavy water. I put a finger out to a letter coaxing a droplet to flow. It is quiet, no sound of the fifty women, struggling, praying, working escapes the walls.

My pressure on the buzzer is answered immediately, I feel a flip-flop of pleasure as I cross the foyer to the small grill set beside the large wooden drum. "Mark! . . . oh Sister Mark! . . . we didn't know when to expect you . . .

Oh, Reverend Mother will be so pleased . . . how was your trip? . . . was it bumpy? Oh what am I doing keeping you standing there, I'll get the keys. Be right back." I listen to the scurrying on the other side of the wall and the bells ringing for the second person necessary for the opening of the cloister doors.

There in the silent empty foyer I recall how frightened I was of the dark wooden structure of the turn; expecting somehow, when it revolved and its opening faced outward, to be face to face with a fat smiling demon licking his chops. Da-da, da da da . . . the hollow within rumbles when I rap on the wood. I do a blues staccato, then, changing the beat, rap an aaba sixteen bar chorus. I am just getting warm when a loud cough interrupts my jazz.

"Well, you're back," Sister Reginald's dour tones sift through the wall like soil creep. Keys rattle against metal. Smells of tallow, greenery, cinnamon and wax flow over me as the cloister door opens and I step through the cubicle we call the speakeasy. I'm home, I think. I'm home! I rap gently on the empty innards of the turn in passing.

The heavy woolen habit falls into place piece by piece, and as each piece descends—tunic, habit, headbands, toque, veil, scapula—I am aware of the mind change that occurs with the "religious weeds," as we called them in the novitiate.

When the clapper sounds for Vespers I file into my accustomed place, returning surreptitious smiles and nods. We're like a flock, I think, the V opens for those who have been working in the birthing clinics, firming up ranks without missing a beat when they return from class and work.

Full of gratitude, I make the requisite sign to ask Reverend Mother Damian for permission for a penance in the refectory, before the evening collation. She nods formally, then, leaning forward, hugs me.

All wait to begin the office. The chapel is still. The candles flicker. The slate roof high overhead registers the metallic click of hail. Poinsettias have been placed on the main church altar, you can just make out the tips of the plants from the choir stalls. Christmas in the cloister! The liturgy is joyous, each week of Advent bringing a lightening of penance. There is expectancy in the most suspicious breast. And last, but far from least, the kitchen sisters outdo themselves! It is calorie time!

Lying prostrate at the door to the refectory while the community steps one by one over my body, I lose my sense of unworthiness, my sense of gratitude slips away. I am distracted by the heavy habits. I am counting fewer than a dozen women wearing the modified skirt. Drag . . . drag . . . drag of heavy wool over my shoulders. Must be the holidays, I think, nose throbbing against the hard flooring. In the month I've been away there has been an appreciable return to the classical habit.

"Are they really as good as they say?" " What are the hill people like?" "The old midwives must know a thing or two!" "How much folk medicine is practiced?" "Do they use herbs?" "Non-interventionist, at the very least they must be." "It would be a joy to use your God-given sense again . . . this wading through fetal monitors and 'gram' machines . . . fighting the probable lawsuit, and the lawyer, to get to the baby."

"Sisters, sisters!" Reverend Mother has heaved upward in her armchair at the end of the room, "give her time to breathe. Sister Mark has a week's vacation, plenty of time to answer all our questions." The women in the room settle down with good-natured grace; there is rustling as sewing is picked up, filing cards and boxes pulled forward, repairs baskets uncovered.

"I'm new of course," my voice falters for just a moment, the old stage fright returning before so many expectant faces, "the school seems to be in some turmoil."

Sister Reginald speaks, "I don't think you should have moved off campus."

"Well, it really isn't a campus, it's . . . "

"Doesn't matter, you live in community here . . . there's a community there, you should live in it. How sane can it be to have a religious living up some 'hollar' as you call it, alone?"

Reverend Mother has been sharing my letters, "I'm not alone."

"You live with someone?"

"Not really, but there are good people nearby." I see Reverend Mother, in that peculiar Janus fashion of hers, watching me with one eye and the community with the other. I gather courage. "I did not want to live away from the dorm, truly I didn't. I tried, I couldn't live a life of prayer in that dormitory."

A sigh of understanding heaves in the room like a Tsunami. Sister Reginald looks away, then back. Reverend Mother's shoulders relax.

"You did well then to move!" Sister Marita's thin eighty-six year old voice lays the matter to rest.

In the silence that follows, Sister James, her round face florid, calls across from her seat, "What about their birthing practices?"

"What I've seen isn't encouraging. But, we haven't seen much, yet."

"What have you been doing?" someone asks.

"Preparing for culture shock," I laugh.

Culture shock . . . culture shock . . . the whisper goes around the group, neighbor asking neighbor . . . did she say, "culture shock?"

"You're not in Mozambique!" Barnabas is wide-eyed.

"I know!" Their silence tells me they are waiting for me to enlarge on this. I begin, "there seems to be a wall between the townspeople and hospital hill. We're warned continually about the strange and sometimes backward ways of the people."

"They have been there longer than you have, maybe they know something you don't." Sister Reginald's dour voice breaks through my preoccupation. "I suspect it's difficult being a student again," a self-satisfied smile plays around her lips.

"Maybe." I sigh forcing myself to remain calm.

"No, there's something else going on . . . " I sit for long moments searching . . . "a bad piece of brain washing, that's what it is!" A phrase of Jean Cocteau's rises before my inner ear, "Mystery is always spun out when hypocrisy can feast itself in the name of humanness." That's too oblique. I try to pick up the thread for my sisters, I don't want to give a wrong impression. I talk about the mountain, Dan and Tempi, Hurl, Vasti and the children, how warm and funny they are. They laugh.

"See! you are among Christians, you will come to no harm, I think she did very well finding that cabin, Mother, don't you?" Sister Benedict looks to Mother Damian.

At the end of recreation period, the clapper for great silence sounds and the community files off to their individual cells . . . to work, read, pray . . . wait for the bell for the first hours of the next day's Divine Office. Reverend Mother has told me she will see me in the morning. The cell is cold, both sections of window are frosted; the textured ice tapestry flickers as the wind swings the light in the garden below. The wind has picked up, I am home but I am far from equilibrium. What mystery is being spun out at Saddleback?

"Sometimes an idea insinuates itself. Because it does so forcefully doesn't make it a right idea." Reverend Mother is sitting in the stiff-backed chair by her desk. I have pulled up a low bench and hunker down on it, elbows on knees. The sleet has changed to fine confectioner's snow which we are watching accumulate in the squirrel's nest in the high section of the oak.

"I needed to hear you expand on some of the very

real misgivings you did not touch on last night. Interesting about the cabin, it will be a saving . . . that it should turn up when you needed it . . . interesting."

I am quiet. I have said all I wanted to say and have been heard, this is such a release that I feel light as a pinch of down. When she asks me about the "other matter" I discard the flip comment that comes only too rapidly to my lips and answer seriously.

"I OD'd before a psychiatrist one day, but I don't think he noticed." Her eyebrows climb. "He said something beautiful, but I don't think he noticed that either. He said we would be alright when we embraced uncertainty. The golden one was out of her cave at the tip of my spine like a bolt," I smile, remembering.

We are still for awhile. Then, "Sebastian could use help in the library. A parishioner came into an inheritance that included some books. A truckload was deposited at the maintenance gate last week. She said they were 'godless,' but maybe we could use them." Reverend Mother sighs. "I told her we had no use for secular/pornographic literature, but she replied they were 'godless,' not pornographic."

The scriptorium is ablaze, it takes my breath away to see the very air glow in the light from the amber cylindrical windows. Before the mansion was given to the church, the owner's wife converted the ballroom on the second floor into a chapel. What had been a vestry behind the high altar now holds two easels, a drafting table, an assortment of stools and a wide L-shaped desk. And golden light. When the chapel became too small for the community, fund raising was begun for the church on the ground floor. Eventually the chapel became the library, my favorite place.

Leaving the rainbow light of the library's stained glass windows, I carry the thirteenth and final carton through the door of the scriptorium, aware of Sisters Patrick and Angelica's discernable sigh of relief at the long table. I close the door gently, drop my skirts and scapula from their tucked position under my belt and get to work.

Squat, stacked guardians, the boxes circling the desk leave little room to move. I lift one and begin bringing books out, laying them face up in the yellow light. Down the L and across I go and reaching the end, form another line, chevron-like, off to the edge again.

The available space is rapidly filled. I decide to subdivide. I put James Mellaart's, *Catal Huyuk* published by McGraw Hill atop Stylianos Alexiou's, *Minoan Civilization*. Vincent Scully's, *The Earth . . . Greek Sacred Architecture* published by Yale University Press seems to go with Annette Laming's *Lascaux: Painting and Engraving,* and Heinrich Zimmer's, *The Art of Indian Asia* and Edith Parada's, *L'art le monde.*

William James' *Religious Experience* sits nicely on top of Mircea Eliade's, *History of Religious Ideas* and Alexander Marshack's, *Roots of Civilization.*

Barbara Walker's, *Woman's Encyclopedia of Myths and Secrets* goes riding on Merlin Stone's, *Ancient Mirrors of Womanhood* and *When God Was a Woman.* The next book is Robert Briffault's, *The Mothers.* I wave it around in the air indecisively, finally dropping it on Kerenyi's, *Goddesses of Sun and Moon.*

The stack on Goddesses grows so high I start another on the floor. Sibelle Von Cles-Redon's, *The Realm of the Great Goddess;* O. G. S. Crawford's, *The Eye Goddess; Lady of the Beasts* by Buffie Johnson; *The Great Mother* by Erich Neumann.

The desk is definitely listing. I put everything on myth on the floor, some twenty books. Starting another subdivision I place Starhawk's *Truth or Dare* and *Spiral Dance,* and *The Holy Book of Woman's Mysteries* by Zsuzanna Budapest, on top of *Women at the Well* by Kathleen Fisher, and cover that in turn with *Descent to the Goddess* by Perera.

So these are the "godless" books. Someone collected a library on ancient religion, primarily Goddess-oriented. Throw in a dozen or more books on Wicca and you have someone who owed no allegiance to a Father-God.

There are studies on digs and anthropological sites—two look like thesis reports—two yellowed articles on new finds in obscure temples, portfolios of pictures on serpent mounds and earth works, and a series of hand diagrams of Catal Huyuk, a seven thousand year old site in modern Turkey.

Gathering the diagrams and putting them to one side I sit back and begin reading. Two of the articles are rebuttals of the thesis reports, quality paper, print sharp, prose systematic in elucidating loopholes in the data. And yet. I go back over the dissertations, a warm glow spreading. The spokesperson in the gut! Attributing weight, here, removing it, there. I watch the muting of the yellow in the room as cloud ceilings lower. I am remembering a drab, overcast day, the coldest part of winter last.

I hurry over the long cleared path through the garden to the storage shed/garage up against the fence, pulling close the large, brown wool coat. My bell, one long, six short, ..., pulls me from work I have uneasily been doing, waiting my turn, my speaking part in the drama of Apostolic Visitation. "Be honest," Mistress of Novices says.

Opening the heavy door I think of the Holy Father, his love for contemplatives, his concern they be allowed to live and pray in peace, for the greater good. In the history of The Church, there most certainly has been abuse, but not here, not in this house. No need to worry. No need to fear someone sent by The Congregation of Religious.

I take a deep breath. A thin man, dark hair, black suit, turned collar, nods to me from the chair on his side of the close-spaced bars and spikes. "Please sit down." The voice is dusty. Hooded grey eyes watched me from their sallow folds as I shed the communal coat and sit and face him in the single, straight chair this side of the massive grillwork. He turns the pages of a ledger lying before him on the table. "You are Sister Mark? Sister Teresa Mark?"

"Teressa Mark, yes, Father."

Bored eyes looked at me, "Do you know why I'm here?"

"Yes Father." A warm, gentle wave of air from the purring heater on his side laps at my face. I relax a little. What a job. Sure an he'll be well fed the three days he's here, housed comfortably enough in the extern quarters, but who on earth would want this, this travelling from monastery to monastery in search of perversions and mishandling of authority.

The poor man looks tired, almost gaunt. Maybe he's sick. Maybe he isn't fit for other work. So this is the Apostolic Visitor; he does not feel ensouled.

"Would you say you were happy here, Sister?" the voice is low and I have to lean forward.

I hesitate only an instant. "Yes, Father."

There is a long pause. "Who in *your* family wanted *you* to become a nun?" A wan, colleagial smile flirts with his thin lips.

I am perplexed. "No one."

"Come now, Irish-Catholic . . . they love the idea of having a religious in the family."

"Well . . . no, not really . . . they think it's throwing my life away, Father."

"Humph . . . humn." He looks at the ledger. "You're somewhat older than most applicants, Sister. Lived a full life in the world?"

I am caught off guard. "Full" would be one way of describing it.

"Dating?"

"Dating?"

He nods, "any problems there? Don't miss all that do you? Men, friends, clothes, travel . . . " He smiles, a rueful, thin smile. "Wouldn't want anyone to think you were running, couldn't handle the world and all . . . " It is an effort at jocularity. It fails. I smile. I shake my head in the negative. I support his effort.

"We are not always honest about our reasons for acting. Would you agree, Sister?"

"I, I try to be honest, Father." I am trying at that minute to keep an up-beat profile in the face of the heavy joylessness sifting through to me. For fifteen minutes, following protocol unknown to me, we have been talking. Or, I have been talking. He has been asking.

"Well, I would like to return to the reason you gave as to the impetus, the motive," he coughs, "the impulse that brought you to religious life. 'A voice told me' . . . I did not want to interrupt you then, but I wish you would address yourself to this." Wrinkling up his nose he scratches and pulls an ear lobe.

"I didn't mean an actual *voice*, Father. Although . . . in many ways . . . it's more Real than much of what passes for reality."

The priest sighs deeply.

A little alarm rings in my heart. I have spoken at great length and with great love of contemplative prayer but I have, from long experience, become cautious and I've carefully refrained from mentioning the light-energy coiling up my spine.

"You say you were told you should enter. This is the 20th century, we are a little more aware . . . You've spent a lot of time in solitary prayer, Sister. Started as a young girl, daily meditation, vigils, retreats when you had the chance . . . all that," he finishes it off with a cut of his hand. A bemused expression softens the furrows on his forehead, "we build our own worlds, Sister, write our own parts, act them. Our pride is deadly when it is unperceived. Once you recognize how inadequate you are in your human frailty you begin to see the extent of the pride in us."

I am in turmoil at his words. I don't know what to say. I have no name for the inner Reality, the knowing that springs from the core. The core which in my secret dialogues I don't know whether to address as

God, Goddess, Nameless One, Lord/Lady, Love. All of these? Have I been gullible and naive? But, I never thought to name it . . . pride. This conflict, this curdling at his words, does it indicate there is unpleasant truth in what he is saying? I do not speak.

"Sister." His voice pulls me back to the speakroom chair. He is leaning forward across the table. "Sister, I'm not asking you to live without your counsel, your *voices*." The words are fatherly, gently exasperated. "I'm asking you to look in your heart, realize how subjective, how fallible are our personal guides. You must see this already, this is why you are taking a vow of obedience." He smiles and nods, "For us, there is surety in this vow. As religious, the chain of authority is *gold*. The Superior is the lifeline to the Infinite."

He sits in silence. When he speaks the dusty voice has changed. Benign, rounded edges strike me. "Always God, through the Order's Constitution and the voice of your Reverend Mother, Sister. It's a matter of priority. You must search your heart. Where does your allegiance lie? It isn't done in a day, or a week, or a year, but the sure way of obedience is the way to topple the ego and loosen pride's hold. It is the only way for us."

Lying on my plank bed after clapper sounds lights-out that night, I feel like Peter after he had denied The Lord. I should have said more? I didn't present a defense? But, what of his questions? An unsettling chill fills my body and I shiver under the coarse wool. Is it unmitigated pride that deceives me into thinking I have a wobbly but sure line to the infinite? I lie awake for a long time.

It has grown quite dark in the scriptorium. Why should I remember that? Why should I remember it *now*? A snorty laugh escapes me. I haven't succeeded in quieting the inner voice, haven't succeeded in loosening pride's hold. Is it ego then that gives the thesis reports this weighty rightness? The bell for Vespers rings.

Returning forty-five minutes later I pick up where I left off. I am engrossed, all my attention focused on sketches of a birthing room painted red, used by women on the Anatolian plain thousands of years ago, when that most extraordinary sensation at the base of my spine turns over and wakes. Curling, spiraling, pushing radiant energy through the spinal column into my head, the whirlwind flows.

For better or worse, I've devised my own unholy, or schizophrenic method of dealing with the rising rotation of this light/energy. I laugh. Call it polarity-therapy. Life must go on. I am a tenuous response to some curious evolutionary principle; since the greater picture is denied me, I accept that Wisdom knows what She is doing, but that doesn't mean I must relinquish everything else.

No, when the baby (my normal everyday life) is in danger of being thrown out with the bath water, something in my Celtic background rebels. If Spirit wants to flower in the flesh, fine, just as long as the body continues and life goes on. I lecture myself not to be enthralled. This always makes me laugh. Laughter is followed by subsequent muting of attention.

If I am successful, if I move fast enough, the golden one cannot overspread my brain's awareness. The river of light subsides and withdraws slowly back down to the cave. It doesn't always work, today it does, I want very much to continue reading. With the diffuse attention that functions best at times like this, I turn back to Catal Huyuk.

CHAPTER 8

The relief I experience at the end of the dark bumpy ride from the airport is very real, the blaze of hospital lights, welcome. Re-routed all over the Midwest because of fog, I feel like an airport zombie.

There is no phone at the cabin, the company took my deposit but couldn't say when. There are twenty parties on the line. Vasti warns me it doesn't pay to be on it, ye can never use it, she says.

Parking the Ford in the deserted hospital parking lot, I head for the phones in the lobby to call Reverend Mother. A summons in the dark. Someone has turned off all the lights and only the tiny baseboards glow beneath the phone booths against the far wall, like teeth in the center of a black expanse. Slowly, I walk toward the shadowy back wall.

There are no active phones. The operator says the lines were shot out between here and Serendipity. There is unrepressed glee in her voice, "Had quite a party they did, got to feudin 'n' one thing led to another . . . before they knew it the lines were plumb blown away."

Early morning, I am sipping cold, fresh water from the well, having just filled my jugs. "Y'lavalat y'lavaleak." Hurl's arm gesture as he strides by is in the direction of the Pinto. It's the arm motion that gives the hint. The verbal could be a shepherd calling for his sheep.

Breathing deeply in the fresh, cold air I find myself grinning up at the neat spiral of smoke from my roof. It's fanciful, but looking at the cabin balanced on its poles, hanging out over the steep slope, I think of seafaring peoples, homes on stilts, waves lapping.

There's no doubt about it, the left rear tire is flat, and the large wet area on the dirt under the front end smells of gasoline. I change the flat, and when I have finished, poke around under the hood. I cannot believe my good luck and hurry to the house to get what I need to repair the crack my finger has found in the hose.

My bottom is making self-satisfied rounds in the dirt when Hurl walks by again. "Find it?"

"Yup."

"Fix it?"

"Bandaid." He laughs and continues on his way.

First official day of class. While I slept, the sky let four inches of powder fall. The white bunting on the slant roof of the outhouse gives a little sigh as it adjusts to the quickened pace of the snow. The car tires make squeegee sounds as I drive out of the hollow. The remnants of skeletal timbers jutting above the gaping hole of the mine . . . the escaping steam, just like a cauldron I think, rolling down the window to listen for sounds of traffic.

Feeling the blacktop take over I slow the speed of the car even more and make the first turn before the descent carefully. It is very quiet, muffled really, I shoot a quick look out over the valley before turning into the second curve.

It all happens so fast. There is a chrome bumper in front of me and my tires are dancing on silk or oil. A freeze around my heart, I brake lightly. The Pinto gives a lurch. One moment I am heading for the thousand foot drop. The next, I am sliding sideways.

The edge of the cliff passes by on my left. The car pulled gently but steadily by the incredible slope of the road is in frictionless glide down the mountain.

I suddenly realize we haven't hit. The truck and I, a mere six inches apart, are doing a shimmy/dance routine, in suspended silence. I can't see the cab, just the immensity of grey bumper. I know from the jockeying of the chrome this way and that, he is straightening out his cab with many necessary corrections on the wheel as he drives backward away from me.

At the bottom I sit with my mouth open, breathing . . . in . . . out . . . in . . . out. The truck pulls its large left front tire up to my window, "You OK?" the voice is young and gruff. I try to say something but all I can do is shake my head while trying to control the chill that ripples through me. "Knew ya cunna stop," he hesitates, "sure yer OK?" It is a few moments before I can resume control of the car and drive the rest of the way into Relief.

Embroiled in what is euphemistically called "Intensives," my left ear is inflamed and my breasts feel like bread dough gone flat from too much working. From eight a.m. until six or seven p.m., three days out of five, we hammer on each other. Sphygmomanometers, otoscopes, opthalmoscopes, tuning forks . . . we use them.

Ester, pounded and pricked to distraction finally rolls herself into a ball, bare butt flashing, and tumbles heels over head the length of the room, "I'm normal, I'm normal," she shouts.

Allison, who has me for a patient, is giving me her most pensive look, "I see angioid streaks in your retina." At the end of the day I am exhausted. And we have weeks of this!

The logs of the cabin are cracking like woods in deep winter. Soup bubbles on the cook-stove, coal bombards the innards of the heat stove, firing tiny rockets and finally settling down.

In-depth lectures by one of the house physicians have started, along with classes by a psychiatric social worker, and the community organizer administrator whose vibes bother me so. Every day Mrs. Kane hands out more modules that have to be "mastered." The pressure is increased incrementally.

My head is full of cell function, protein synthesis and transport, membrane potential, neuronal synapsis; subatomic particles in a bubble chamber couldn't be more intriguing, I love it!

It is difficult. I see why some women come early to take this one course, but I love it. The amazing mystery, science of the human body, the play, the dance! Too bad the course is on video, it makes it unnecessarily difficult. An instructor comes periodically from Lexington to review and to answer questions.

There is a timid knock on my door as I sit musing by the stove, I push the latch up and swivel in my seat. Vasti's soft brown eyes repeat the "Hope I'm not bothering." I follow her across the slope.

"I stop a tha front desk an tha cashier she say I owe forty dollar, forty dollar! I say, I dinna cum ta buy the hospital, I cum ta hav summon look at my boy's foot. Forty dollar!" he repeats the round figures in disbelief. "They jus soak it," he shakes his head, "I say ta her, tha can na be forty dollar!"

The angrier he gets, the less the rolling hills surface. I understand him clearly. Hurl's eyes are matt black, he stomps back and forth, back and forth, devouring the room's air, belching it back at the bloated walls.

I sit with the heel of Harlin's foot on my knee; king of the hill, his eyes and Michael's follow their Dad with rapt attention. "There's a piece of quilting needle in thar." Vasti sighs. She speaks with enforced calm even as she nods agreement with Hurl.

He is reciting a tale of bureaucracy, mischarge, long waits, itemizing to the point of ridiculousness, student clinicians, "Tha doan know more than ya do when ya cum." He punches a fist into his palm, "Can afford it, doan need it!"

I have been gently prodding the blue balloon of a toe. "Doan hurt," Harlin proudly wiggles it from side to side as Michael watches. There are no tell-tail red fingers, it's localized. I need to get something, I put the boy's foot down gently and walk back to my cabin.

While I soak the foot Vasti talks about the grief of "havin tha hospital up thar." A year to pay for Michael, she says. All the rest were born at home without a single problem, "they doan charge you fer toothpaste at home!"

When I ask her why she didn't have Michael at home as well, she looks at me with troubled eyes, "They say thas not a good idea now." Hurl has calmed down and has pulled up a chair, "Didn use ta be like this," he says apologetically. He seems more confused than angry now.

"How come you let to me, I mean, feeling like you do?"

"Doan care fer em, doan av anythin agin ya." His eyes crinkle.

I give him the flashlight to hold while I look for glitter from the broken quilting needle under the magnifying glass. "I can't see it. We're going to continue soaking . . . and in between soaks," I open the lid of the ointment and, scooping a hefty dollop crown the toe with the black snowball.

"Whas that?!"

"Cow balm," I say in deep stentorian tones and turning to Hurl, "if he gets red streaking you've gotta take him . . . "

"I'm not going back thar!" he interrupts me.

"Serendipity then . . . take him to Serendipity."

The worlds revolve like ancient women gathering fuel in vacant lots . . . I can't remember who said that. I've never been in a situation like this. Our instructor, Tandera Kane, fills a room full of audiovisual equipment and mockups of the human body. And leaves. We eye each other, who knows anything about breasts, someone asks. I do. We huddle over the intraductal tumor. Has anyone been exposed to rebound associated with lung infiltrate? This video is very confusing. Yes, Becky moves across, she's worked anesthesiology for two years.

Our new Pediatrics instructor, Miss D., arrives to the minute. She doesn't look at us, she never smiles. She spreads her material on the table, arranges it into piles, breaks these down, lays it all out again, breaks it down . . . until, finally satisfied, she glances over our heads at the clock. "Shall we begin?" It is not a question.

The hospital administrator decides we should do a class project as well as the required individual one. We are silent. More make-work. I try to be objective about the feeling I get in close proximity to this man. How does one "feel" a lie? It is unsettling. It is hollow. To sit near him is to swallow a bucketful of ice.

Three a.m.. The cold is biting. The weeks are flying by. The stove is out again, an airtight it is not! The floor creaks as I jump from the bed, pull on socks, heavy robe, slippers. I look like a zebra streaked round with coal.

Might as well review for the three exams today. There used to be an honor system, but no more, not after "last year's cheating." Now we sit our exams under watchful eyes and only at assigned times.

There is so much pressure on it is almost impossible to clear the mind for any kind of prayer; term papers, projects, studies, tests . . . like a graveyard emptying, macabre puppets vie for attention.

Oh, Mother, help!

A half hour later, I can begin. A half hour later I am full of peace. Marvelling at how quiet the cemetery is, I make coffee and settling up in the loft at the desk, begin work.

CHAPTER 9

Warmth! I feel I've died and gone to heaven. The shower stall at the rear of the nurses' locker room is full of steam. I turn, letting the spray pelt my back, neck and shoulders.

For days I've had no heat at "owl." For days, long days, beginning in dark, ending in dark, I've had smoke, but no appreciable heat. And no time to wrestle with a recalcitrant stove. Did I put the damper in right? Could it possibly have gotten clogged so soon? Had I been burning green wood I could understand this, but coal? I don't know anything about the black stuff. The cabin walls may as well be paper, sixteen degrees outside, it must be twenty within; exposed above and below in my tree house, I'm too weary to contend with it all!

I can smile a little at it now, but an hour ago huddled in my coat, drinking hot cocoa, eyes smarting and almost useless, trying to memorize: smiles, coos, gains hand control, reaches with arm, rolls over, sits alone, crawls . . . for a growth and development quiz, I felt like crying.

I feel sinfully extravagant letting the hot water run like this, but, oh! I am beginning to revive. At six a.m. there is evidently no one around, not even a sign of housekeeping; administrative offices dark and empty, classroom section deserted.

As if blown by a puff of air the shower stall bellows softly. Someone must have come into the locker room. Rousing myself—it is time, I tell myself—to get my act together, I turn the handle from full on to off.

The nozzle empties, a small waterfall, then drip, drip. The steady drip spaces itself as I reach around for the towel, straining in the warmth for the noise that will identify the other person in the large room. All is quiet outside the stall.

There should be some noise I think, feeling curiously edgy, remembering the emptiness and darkness of the halls I had passed through. Drip . . . drip . . . then, yes! there, I hear wheels turn. The housekeeping cart has wheels like that, my back relaxes.

I am sitting clothed on the narrow bench, tying my no-nonsense athletic shoes, when I hear the rustling. Away at the front of the locker room I hear the bump of a metal pail, then the swing of a toilet stall door . . . and closer, much closer, a rustling.

Shush-shush . . . shush-shush . . . shush, the disembodied straw sound has approached the closed door at my elbow. And stopped. Someone is sweeping the floor, nothing unusual about that . . . but even as I tell myself this I realize that there are no human vibes coming from the other side of the door, there is a soft rustling but no foot sounds. Mother of God! I am getting punchy, and with that, I open the door outward.

No bird goddess, no phallic symbol with a hole in its head . . . a broom, a sturdy, simple broom waits in my path; my knuckles grazing the wood, it wobbles ever so slightly, sways, and rights itself. I am dumb. Then, in a delayed reaction, starting at my heels, all the hair follicles on my body fill out and rise.

A quilled animal, I panic. My eyes search wildly for a human, fear screaming silently around the walls, and as if the fear reaches her, Iah pops out of one of the cubicles, mop and pail in hand.

Taking in the scene she walks calmly down the valley of lockers toward me, reaches for the broom as if it is exactly where she hoped she'd find it, and smiles. The eyes meeting mine are full of peace and well-wishing but I feel like a child that has somehow failed a test.

"Upon a pole, a hawk. And how is thee, woman who sleeps in the Lady house?" She's not a good looking woman. Her nose has been broken in at least two places and it has healed like the slash and dash signs on a typewriter. She is slender to the point of skinniness, wiry, I guess she'd call it. Her vibes are good. She looks humorous enough to be real.

Does it matter then, that she catches errant brooms and tucks them like wayward children under a protective arm? I don't know what to think, but as I look from her to the broom the quills lie down and my breathing slows.

"Well, how are ye doing in the wee house of ancestral spirit?" her smile widens. When I don't answer she leans over and gently pats my hand, "doan ye worry, where they's fear, they's power."

"Iah . . . " I haven't the slightest idea what to say about the broom, so I don't. "I was having trouble with the stove, can't get it to work right, was near froze, so much smoke, it's been so cold . . . " I babble on.

"Here, here, cum sit," we walk back together to the alcove before the line of lockers where two old armchairs squat. "Now tell me, how ye like livin in our hill?"

We are the same age. She has lived in the Minneapolis area, since that was where work could be found, but felt she was dying in the city and came back to her "tucky hill."

We have been talking for about ten minutes when the main doors are thrust open and four upper class women bustle in. She gets quickly up as they eye us and, bending ostensibly to retrieve her pail, whispers, "I will think on the stove." Winking, she goes to her cart.

"That was sweet," R. B. has caught up with me in the hall.

"What?"

"I mean, it's really nice to see you talking to the staff. More should do that." I hunch my shoulders. "You should come to the Student Senate meetings, it helps to blow off steam."

"Do you wish to take over the class!?" Mrs. Kane's eyes are bulging and her voice shaking with anger.

"Uh . . . no, I only thought, I thought I could simplify for Sue . . . " Ann's face is flushed.

"I suggest you keep quiet, we have a lot of work to cover."

There it is, "cover" not learn. I feel sorry for this middle aged woman. The job is evidently too much for her; she is no teacher and, as a result, jealously guards every ounce of her supposed authority.

Some of my classmates have extensive updated knowledge. Lynn for one has worked for a neurosurgeon for the past two years. While she is lecturing, Tandy will allow no reciprocal sharing, logjams of questions produce looks of uneasiness, a re-reading of the text, then out-and-out belligerence. "We must move on!" she says. We whisper the answer, write notes in the margins of our pads, pass them to our neighbors, who pass them surreptitiously on.

Our unsmiling Pediatrics instructor, Miss Penelope Privis, is half Tandy's age. I don't think I've ever encountered a younger woman so rigidly under control. It's a long day!

At five p.m. the door separating our class from the administrative offices is closed. We look at one another waiting for someone, anyone, to take the lead. We are one in frustration and anger, what to do?

"This is unbelievable." Lynn's words are statement of fact, but the eyes she raises to the group are uncomprehending.

"We've got to go to the dean!"

"No," Ann answers, "the Student Senate!" The ice is broken. Huge cakes move into the flow. "We must get another instructor, Kane is useless!" "A month-long orientation, and for this! I can't believe it!" "Grade point averages . . . baseline excellency measuring systems . . . if I hear one more word about the number that don't make it I'll scream!" "The last class sure did have a problem with T.K. . . . and it wasn't a personality problem!" "I want to scream during her lectures!" "She's hopeless, how about going to the dean?"

"Mark, you're the oldest, would you go for us?" Yes, I'm the oldest, I think, and that means I've been here, in this very same position before . . . and when I stood as spokeswoman, I turned to find I stood alone.

"I would go as part of a group, yes! I definitely would go to the dean with you."

"I think we should grit our teeth and get on with it." Everyone turns to look at Ester.

"Yeah, I think we should ignore it, just get through and get the hell out of the place," Beverly is nodding vigorously.

"But we have to stand up for our rights," Erin's eyes are huge, "we should have a sit down."

"How about going to the dean right now,?" I wait for them. Two say they have something to do. One says she has to study. One says she has heard the dean doesn't like people dropping in on her, she wants appointments made.

At the open door of the now empty conference room, Erin and Lisa watch me, "Well, there's no way we can go just the three of us," they say. A passing senior student glances at us, "Aha! methinks the new class is in the throes of culture shock!"

Her moons artifice . . . I walk the path under a crisp waxing moon. I am not a poet, I don't know where to go with the words, but from beginning to bless, I know imperceptible modulations of white light. The hollow is drenched in silver as I return home this night.

My eyes follow the delicate crystal sound that is making minute inflections on the crisp air and follow it up the slope to the porch of the cabin. I don't know what I'm looking at. I climb closer.

When I am level with the porch I put out a hand and touch. At two foot intervals, all along the overhang of roof, huge glittering icicles hang. Catching the light, under the gentle wind, they thrum, crystal organ pipes creating fairy song.

To get inside I'll have to break them, where on earth did they come from? My house is a glitter cage, an ice castle. I've never seen anything like it. My gloved hand damps a high trill, I gaze stupidly upward, the sound winging past my eyes, and see the smoke. A hefty curl of smoke rises from my stove pipe. It is the first hefty curl I've seen in many days. And the ice. The ice can be attributed to leakage. The cabin is leaking like a sieve.

Putting my book bag on the porch, taking two three-foot icicles in hand, I break them off and open the door. Heat waves on my face. Behind the isin-glass of the coal stove a level layer of smokeless blue glows. I stare at it.

Pulling the rocker over, I sit. Quite possibly the layer of smoking coal caught after I left this morning, burning the plug out of the chimney. Because it was a good thick layer, quite possibly it reached its stride and settled down to burn like it should.

Quite possible. But I don't believe it. I get up and wander. I poke a finger in half a dozen plants and find the dirt no longer cold. The wet towels I left hanging are all dry. The room behind the kitchen, the "cold room" where I store my water jugs, is warm, and the water in the jugs is unfrozen.

Marvelling, and in need of movement, I take the jugs outside, empty the stale contents on the ground and descend the slope to the well.

The stones enclosure is a dark round eye in the moon-splashed hollow. Unhooking the bucket, I thrust it with decision into the center of the sixteen foot well and listen to the supple rebound as it hits the surface way below, eddys, and tips to fill down at the black, cold moving bottom.

I'm learning. I'm learning to draw water, my buckets no longer bobbing around on surfaces like floating barges. Inaudible combinations of pull and tug inform my arm muscles that the bucket is full.

Hand over hand, I haul, ripple-arm, shoulders easy, keeping to the center so as not to snag on the offset stone. Without losing a drop, I ease the bucket onto the wide smooth lip. One by one I fill the jugs, never believing I could be so happy simply hauling water in moonlight.

CHAPTER 10

A whirling dervish splicing remnants of time for some little bit of relationship and sharing, I feed the stove, bag my dirty wash, stick my last bottle of wine between the shirts and socks, drive back into town and on up the hill to Wednesday cottage, fill the washing machine, help set the table, prepare a salad, and collapse weary but satisfied, to listen to the little professor from the university talk in chemical equations and essential elements.

Reviewing the past weeks' video, she asks for questions. The casserole is delicious, the wine is delicious, there are no questions. She starts telling stories of how it was before "that monstrosity was built," gesturing with contempt down the darkened slope to the thirty bed hospital. "A sad day, the one we didn't pass fire inspection," she says.

After everyone has left, Rose helps me fold my wash. "You don't have to you know."

"Oh, yes, I know . . . I just . . . " her voice trails off.

"Don't want to face the four walls and books yet." I reply for her.

"Yeah, guess." Guess sounds like a gargle and I realize she is crying, tears falling, splat, splat onto the folded sheets.

Taking her in my arms, pulling her toward the double rocker, I sit her down beside me and rock. I rock, rock, rock while she cries.

Wearing a clean lab coat, carrying a black bag heavy with examining tools, I arrive for clinical assignment next morning. Without looking at us, chewing the inside of her mouth, Penny Privis drops three charts, "Here, your patients, two girls and a boy." Ann and Bev take the girls', I pick up the boy's.

The mother wants to come with me and waves goodbye to the girls. The boy bounds after me like an obedient puppy. I stop at the scale to record his height and weight, "Eleven, huh?" he nods, "tall for eleven!" I whistle and he sneaks a look at what I'm writing. He is all loose limbs, bones and gangling joints. Heaving himself up on the examining table he swings his legs and looks around with interest.

"Healthy as a horse," his mother says, "never misses school . . . had a li'l troub with birth, but, he be fine. So many!" she says, a note of panic in her voice as I lay out the forms that have to be filled out, "All we cum fer is a shot."

I give her the answer we have been told to give, "I'm sorry, but they've never been filled out, the record has to be completed."

"How long it gunna take?!"

"Let's get started, see how quickly we can move through it all."

We are one and a half hours filling out forms. I ask her if she would like to go check on the girls, she shakes her head adamantly. "I stay here," she says.

My hands shaking when I finally get around to starting the physical, the casing on the otoscope spins off, two C-cells roll onto the floor and careen away across the room, while the headpiece, ejecting from the light source, lands in the boy's lap. We're not supposed to tell anyone we're new students! I howl with laughter as the boy bolts and comes back to deposit all the interlocking parts in my hands. He is grinning. "I'm new at this," I say, watching the grin widen.

It's a good exam but I'm pitiably slow, it takes me an hour. And then thirty minutes more to get all his shots brought up to the state required levels. Miss Privis puts her head in the room then and tells me she has to repeat the exam.

"Why he av ta av another?" the mother's forehead is creased with worry. As gently as I can I tell her it is the normal procedure because I am a student. Forty-five minutes later, Privis, having finished her examination, leaves the room hurriedly.

"He finish now?" the woman looks weary. I feel weary. Only the boy seems undaunted. Undaunted that is, until Dr. S. appears followed by the entourage of interns and interested students. As the group of strangers crowd into the room, the boy rises on the examining table in panic. Eyes alarmed, he searches wildly around and over the wall of shoulders for his mother who has been forced back against the far wall.

A dilemma? A dilatory learning experience? Pushing through the crowd toward those panic-stricken eyes I reach the end of the table with a lurch that upsets Dr. S.'s arm. He turns angrily, but I am already around the end of the table, the boy's hand in mine. Looking from me to the boy he resumes what he was saying and takes the boy's other arm.

Dr. S. has gone, taking his group with him, the mother and I sit silent while Regel pulls on his jeans. Suddenly there is a crash and a burly-faced man bursts into the room.

"Wha tha hell, womin! wha ya doin?! Wha tha hell ya doin?! I tol ya nod ta bring im here . . . I tol ya . . . I tol ya . . . I tol ya, didn I? didn I tell ya?" Spittle sprays the woman's face before she can get her hands up, "wait'l I git ya home, womin, jus wait!"

Turning, he sees me, "He no need ya, he no need ya ad all, he jus fine!" with that he stomps out, slamming the door. His footsteps echo down the hall. "Doan mind im! thank ye," the woman smiles a tired smile.

I dog Dr. S. until I find him between patients. They want the boy back. Exciting. Although it's still a tentative diagnosis it's a real coup! Fascinating. Wonderful pickup. "There is no cure for what he has," he says, "bet he'll be dead by thirty. We've got a battery of tests to do on that lad."

"Why put the family and boy through it if there's no cure?"

"It's always good to know what people die of," he walks off confidently.

An hour later Penelope Privis is shuffling charts while waiting for the three of us to put finishing touches on the assessment profiles. "You follow that up now, Miss Mark, you keep after that woman, she's got to bring that boy back for those tests. It's a very interesting case, sort of thing you find where there's been inbreeding. If they don't have a phone you'll have to go out there."

"No," the word at first slips out, very softly, very mildly. I am surprised at it landing in the room naked and unprotected.

"What?" She is surprised, too.

"No." This time it's very firm.

"It's your responsibility to keep after that family."

"No, Miss Privis, you do it if you think it's so important, I can't, I won't." Putting down my report, collecting my charts, I file them and start for the door.

"This is going on your record!"

My back toward her, I bunch my shoulders up as I leave.

Ann catches up with me on the tumbled road to Wen, "Did you have to be so hard on her?"

I stop, catching my breath, place two feet wide apart on a level slab of blacktop. "I didn't plan it." I search for understanding in her face, but it is turned down and she makes her way over the rubble.

"Rosalie left this morning. Said she woke up and couldn't find a single reason for staying. Said to tell you she felt great once she made her decision and to wish you luck."

One indian down, I am thinking.

"Are you going to catch the C-section?" she looks back at me.

"Don't have time, after lunch I'm due in adult clinic."

"Don't you just love to see those babies rise up," her voice is happy, "like surprised Buddhas, all perfect, not a mark on them? When Dr. Asiac is on duty, he keeps the OR so cold, the steam pouring from the abdominal cavity makes for a dawn of creation scenario. I tell you the look on their faces is pure surprise."

"Why the C?"

"Usual. Hasn't progressed. She's been in labor ten hours."

Adult clinic is bedlam this afternoon. Mrs. Kane nowhere to be seen. The interns and med students, looking confident, bustle around with charts, beckon people from benches, direct them to examining cubicles.

Eying the confusion, I watch as two men get up from the bench nearest the door, move haltingly to the receptionist's desk and talk to her. The woman's eyes, following the pointing fingers of a hand, move in my direction; nodding at them she waves to catch my attention, her voice carries down the corridor, "Miss?"

When I reach them she peers at my name tag, "sorry, I don't know all your names yet." She is handing me a chart, "this gentleman would like it if you do his exam." I look from her to the men waiting with otherworldly deference, the shorter man is nodding vigorously. The tall emaciated gentleman, all grey coat, skin and hair, leans on his friend's arm.

"My name is Brenner, he's very sick," the stocky younger man searches me with his eyes; the older man, dull and motionless as old pewter, waits trustingly. I touch his hand, it is hot and dry. He attempts a wry smile, croaking, "flu" through cracked colorless lips that curl in a dog's grimace. I forget all about Mrs. Kane, I forget about everything but a soul before me struggling to hold to a disintegrating host.

The interns have been so busy grabbing rooms that I don't know where to take him. As if reading my mind the receptionist leans across the desk, "E is empty, take room E," I smile my thanks.

Peter Olum doesn't mind if his friend stays through the exam and I am grateful for a steady arm. He sits in the chair to the side of the examining table, resting his head on the paper. He follows my instructions weakly as I do the exam right there with him in the chair.

Weight loss, appetite loss, loss of muscle tone, at six foot four he looks like a mold filled with ashen sludge. "He sure it the flu, but Silesia, she say it not the flu."

"Is Silesia his wife?"

"Silesia a witch," there is determination in Peter's

low voice, as if to tell us he can hear quite well and can answer for himself, "fine lady."

Brenner looks over at us, "he wouldna come if Silesia no say he should, she tol us go there this very day! We come," he ends simply.

They watch as I draw ten cc's of dark, red blood from a vein in Peter's arm into a syringe. Brenner holds the stoppers while, removing the needle, I fill each tube. "It's going to take at least an hour for them to finish these tests, I think you should stay right here in the room, it's quiet, no one will disturb you."

On my way through the hospital with the samples I wonder about this person Silesia. Returning, I find them sitting meek as two subdued school boys. "I don't know Silesia," I say.

"She know ya," Peter's cracked voice leaves no doubt. Brenner chimes in, "she know ya, she say look fer ya, she give us yer name," he thrusts his lips out and nods his head.

"Why wouldn't you come until Silesia told you to come, Peter? You've been feeling poorly for weeks?"

His grin is crooked but proud, "I use the potions, they always work . . . before."

"But not this time," I say.

"Silesia didn know he be this sickly, he hide it from er," Brenner interjects, "but Silesia see im!" he shakes a finger at his friend, "she one wise lady! You know herbs?" He's certainly looking more relaxed now that the responsibility for his friend has been lifted from his shoulders.

"I know a little about herbs," I answer.

"Silesia know a lot about herbs and simples, she teach ya."

Leaving them sitting quietly I go in search of Mrs. Kane wondering if she will have to repeat the exam as was done earlier in the day in Pediatrics. I don't find her. Lowering myself into a corner chair in the physician's charting room I review what I've written.

I am aware vaguely of the room filling but I don't look up and the sudden voice at my shoulder startles me, "You ready!? I don't have all day."

It's a perfect imitation of James Cagney playing tough guy, a smile comes to my face, someone's joking around!

I look up. Six or seven serious faces are watching me. The little hippie doctor who wisecracks his way through our in-depth lectures has his face turned as he busies ostensibly with twirling his pen, drumming it hard on the desk. "Come on!" he says, the voice is now angry Cagney. Ten? maybe twenty seconds? I don't know how long it takes me to gulp down the laugh and stand. I know the routine, I've seen it enough. He's for real, at least he thinks he is, and now at this moment that is all that matters.

I marvel at the clarity of my voice and its loudness as I throw it toward the newcomers slipping into the room, "Peter Olum, sixty-four year old, white, unmarried male arrives in clinic 'feeling poorly' claiming he has the 'flu.' Weight loss of thirty pounds in the last six months . . . more recently pallor, debilitating weakness, anorexia . . . "

I refrain from mentioning Silesia. He fires questions at me which I answer. He says, "humph." I am wrapping it up when a girl in a white lab coat waves a slip of paper at me over the heads at the door; it is passed my way.

Sodium . . . chlorides . . . potassium . . . I give the results of the blood chemistries." And the blood sugar is . . . " I catch my breath, "six hundred and eighty."

"Five hundred points above normal!" someone whispers.

"That's it then!" the resident hammers the desk with his closed fist, "admit him!" A swath opens for him, the room empties like a tub with a wide drain. Tandera Kane is the only one left, I hadn't known she was there; "You did good, you did very good!" she says.

My back to the warmth of the stove, I eat my meatless chili, washing down the beans with Rhine wine, while watching a silver moon chin the adjoining ridge; she climbs through the branches of the pine, a girl, a sprite, a will-o-the-wisp almost full. Half over the hill she grins in my window making me restless, or, it could be the beans.

Putting down the bowl, slipping my jacket from its hook, I climb the hill to the outhouse. Best view in the world! propping open the door I adjust to the breeze that roars up the hole.

Can one possess oneself in ambiguity? is that too abstract a question? outhouses with views do this strange thing to me. Something moves around in the preconscious, something for which I have no name; a very tangible inner reality, Arp would say, without meaning, without cerebral intention.

At that moment, a piercing high ululation cuts through the blackness; I am out of the outhouse in a shot, turned north to face it. There it is again, a high, shrill cry, I shiver.

There isn't any wind, it isn't the sound of the wind. Coyote pup? warbling their liquid at the shining in the sky? It descends, moaning lamentation to the depths, then climbs, a pack of hyena, or women in childbirth? Pitched inhumanly high, the warble turns into an ethereal chant, punctuated at intervals with the thud . . . thud . . . thud of a drum.

CHAPTER 11

Even as I tell myself the hollow is full of shadow and rough travelling at night, I am taking my hat, gloves and scarf from the door, and dropping the air vent a notch on the stove. In the black shadow cast by the cabin I pick my way north, relieved to come out into the moonlight after a hundred yards. The land rises darkly in the lee of the curved ridge ahead; I nearly turn back but the chant hits a peak, it definitely isn't in this hollow. And, I'm pretty sure it isn't in the next.

I have been to the ridge at night before, it is rough but if you let your eyes adjust before you have to straddle the gigantic uprooted tree you can shimmy over the low end of the trunk, patting the mother blindly, the damp smell of earth only inches from your nose. The chanting is more subdued here in the overhang.

I am so busy keeping my thoughts on the material plane, denying the unimaginable access, that I forget the boulder shaped like a man that has washed free of the hill. Its sudden rise to my right forces a scream to my clenched teeth. Gaining the summit, my teeth still chattering, I step out in the full thrust of the chant, there are no words just the high pitched incantation.

It is bright up here, every little pebble, every twig, clearly delineated. I walk freely along the packed earth, the ridge-tops in better condition than the roads down below. And turning Northwest at the fork, walk past the large grader that is parked off to one side in the brush.

The moon is so bright that I do not see the glow until I am above the hollow, the strength of the chant trails minute icicles down my spine. For the first time in many days the golden one turns over, yawns and starts to rise.

There is a great bonfire in the hollow below. Sparks ricochet from this and, as I watch, a crooked oak that seems to be leaning a pair of arms out over the fire, seems to be reaching to embrace it. I imagine that I feel the heat on my face although the ridge is too high, the fire too far away.

The boundaries melt. The liquid gold one rises to my waist, moving slowly to the drumbeat. I count fifteen people dancing in the sinuous meander of a circle. The circle is like the one the priest draws around the bread and wine before the consecration of the mass, to enclose the energy of transubstantiation, until, consecration achieved, it is loosed to the world. The rise of light through my spine is otherworldly, I dance, wide open to the cosmos; I dance at the top of the ridge while they dance in the valley below. It is all the same dance.

I am not aware of making unnecessary noise, I am aware I have not lost consciousness; I am unbelievably alert and full of wonderment at the whirl of our particles joining with the moon above. When a woman steps out of the circumference of the circle to the center I am amazed that she points up the hill to me.

"Class on the Immune System postponed until after the meeting with Miss Dulip at 9" . . . the note that greets us as we arrive in the conference room this morning causes an instantaneous festive mood. Anything is better than sitting through Mrs. Kane's tortured classes.

My mind is elsewhere, rethinking the events of the previous night, I do not see Penelope Privis, the Pediatrics instructor, enter the room. "Here," there is a flat plop as the quizzes hit the table. We sort through the pile she has dropped teasing each other lightheartedly.

"Miss Mark, you are behind in your Denver Developmental Studies, the rest of the class has handed in at least six exercises. Some are quite good. I count two from you," she pauses for emphasis.

"I will see to it."

"Before the end of the week, please." I nod.

As soon as she has left the room, "haven't you done your Denvies?! tch . . . tch . . . tch!"

I look at the good natured group of them and laugh, "How did you get them down so fast? I didn't think there were that many kids in town!"

Pointed looks pass between Bev, Diane and Ester . . . "Shall we tell her?" Ester finally bursts out laughing, "we made 'em up."

"You didn't!"

"We did!" more laughter. "But," Ester looks like an undercover agent passing a tip, "if you need a kid or two . . . they hang out in the main lobby during clinic," there is laughter all around

Miss Dulip, Dean of the school, enters the room and the class quiets. She is a woman in her late forties and she would be attractive if it weren't for the dark shadow over her upper lip that gives her a Machiavellian cast.

She nods to us, sits at the head of the table, takes a deep breath and begins. "First I wish to tell you that the school is not closing. Contrary to rumor! In the few months I've been here I've been appalled. Resignations, staff turnover, teacher scarcity . . . student interviews should have been terminated years ago! I can inform you they have been terminated as of now," with this pronouncement she looks each one of us in the eye, looks to see if we are aware of the seriousness of the situation.

"I have convinced the Board that the backlog of midwifery students waiting for birthing experience dictates we stop all admissions as of now."

"Does this mean that we will not have the twenty necessary births nor be eligible to sit certified midwifery boards?" Ester's tone is hard.

"I promise you, you have my word on this, that everyone will get the necessary experience. I'm not sure where, and I'm not sure on what kind of schedule . . . but you *will* get it. We will do all in our power to make sure you get your experience."

Her voice deepens, she shakes her head slowly and settles in her chair. "A school in such chaos!" she shakes her head, "I'd never have accepted a class this size!" She sighs, "we've issued a call to all former graduates, we're looking for people to come and teach for a year. We can't find midwives. They don't exist anymore?! They've gone underground?!"

It is almost as if she is talking to herself. You can hear a paperclip, pushed from the table as she moves her papers, hit the floor. "We could close the midwifery component of the program, phase it out completely. Run the school, base the course work on the Family Practitioner module." A strong murmur of dissent goes around the group. She remembers we're there. Looks at us, the brown eyes suddenly annoyed. "Well, I personally don't agree, we could do quite well simply training Nurse Practitioners. We're exploring many avenues."

Her mouth is covered with her hand so that the following words come out garbled, but they are clear enough. "I have a feeling midwives are more problem than they're worth." She gathers herself together looking very businesslike and forceful. "We promise we will get all enrolled students through, you will get your experience. I'll tell Mrs. Kane I'm finished."

As the door closes behind her someone says, "feel sorry for that woman." This is quickly followed by, "feel sorry for us!"

Sensing the gloom, Tandera Kane wraps up her presentation early, releasing us at eleven-thirty.

I sit undecided as everyone files aimlessly from the conference room. Then, shuffling through my papers and finding blank Denver forms, I head down to the lobby.

Ester is right, the circular room looks like preschool. Three little girls have converted two telephone booths into high-rises; dolls hang from phone hooks, lounge disjointedly in the seats and prop spineless curves against floors and walls. A small boy lies on his tummy on the floor listening to them talk nononsense talk to their children.

Two boys, their sneakers forming half a circle, their socks strung out to complete it, shoot marbles with noisy chortles, glancing surreptitiously at the girls who do not deign to see them. Their bare feet wave about in the air.

A lone boy approaches the boys sprawled watching the girls, "like ta play?" He shows his erstwhile companions how to hop the checkered floor on one leg.

I am heading toward him as the likeliest candidate when a chunky, elderly woman hurries through the double clinic doors. She skirts the two marble players, stumbles on a sock, rights herself and drops her pocketbook.

A shot rings out. An angry whine cuts the air inches from my left ear. A boy drops and rolls yelling, "fire!" A boy covers his head and shouts "riflemen to the right!" then giggles apprehensively. Girls scream. The old woman looks distracted, picks up her pocketbook which is smoking, and walks out the door.

"Wow! jus like Tour of Duty!" the boys are clambering all over the wall to my left. "Hey! here it is! Hey, great! how we gunna dig it out?" No one looks up at my approach, all are watching the boy digging in the wall with his small blade. When they've retrieved the bullet, they turn, "Can we keep it?" And since I am standing there they ask me, "can we?"

"You know what I think?" I wait as the eyes settle down, "I think you should take it to the security cop, I bet he'd be interested in knowing who it belongs to."

"Danny's grandma!" the chorus is unanimous.

"We thought we heard screams." Mary has come through from Emergency, they are falling all over each other in their attempts to tell her. Over their heads she enunciates the words, "anyone hurt, who was it?"

"A little old lady carrying a gun?" my answer is a question.

She grins, probably at the expression on my face, "Everyone carries them around here."

When she leaves to call security I listen to the cacophony . . . and I remember Ester saying, discussing the Denver Developmental Studies, "We made 'em up."

Yeah!

Corded wool drags across the sky in cloud formation at the end of a busy day. A wild twittering of birds has taken up residence in the bush along the creek. A cardinal darts into a V of twiggy brush, a peaked roof of snow at my elbow falls slow-motion like, pattering down on songbird yellow wings below.

Turning from the birds I look ahead on up to the cabin. Then, look closer. Someone is standing on the porch. Rapier thin, silhouette motionless against the lighter sky, someone is watching me.

Not until I am immediately below her do I recognize Iah. "Figure as how it still be light you wooden be frighten," she leans down and takes one of my heavy bags.

"I wouldn't be frightened of you Iah!"

"Yes, I frighten ye, I be sorry about tha. It be lovely here, no?"

"Yes! truly lovely, I'm grateful beyond belief that you knew about the place, couldn't have lasted in the dorm. Four of my classmates are also looking for housing off hospital hill. Will you come in? I'll put the tea kettle on," as I scurry about I wonder why she is here.

I return from depositing my books in the loft to find her pouring a scoopfull of coal in a zigzag pattern among the clinkers on the grate. Back to back with this she drizzles another, where they meet a lick of flame seeps out on either side. "Ya had more troub with tha stove?"

"No." As I put the cups of tea on the table I realize I have not had any trouble since we spoke that morning in the locker room. Suddenly apprehensive, I put a shot glass of brandy next to her cup and a hefty dollop into my mug. I have a swallow of the brew and reassure myself with its warmth before turning. "Iah, are you a witch?"

"Yes." She is pleasantly unconcerned, I could be asking if she owned a green skirt.

I take another swallow, "I, I don't know anything about witches." I cannot see the isin-glass panel on the front of the stove but the coal must flare at that moment, for her eyes flash and the look she fixes on me is piercing.

"It doesna matter wha ye know, it matters wha ye be!" she sips the brandy, then the hot tea. "Brooms doan move, people move thing, I knew ye wer in the locker room tha morn." She cants the shot glass to one side, rolls the amber liquid up to the rim, then tips it back. "I play a lil game, ye take fright. I be sorry!"

"It's alright."

She nods. "This month ye cum, ye doan run well away agin." An uneasy feeling crawls over my skin. "Ye wer on the ridge las moon, ye see us dance the Lady; Ye wer ta cum down, join with us."

I don't know what to say. "Calamus knew ye wer of the wicca, she see the fire when ye dance. She know ye wer cummin ta tha Lady house." There is a soft plaintiveness about the eyes that rest on me, "ye cum? Lady Diane full tonigh."

I am full of confusion, "I have so much work to do Iah, so many papers, tests, projects . . . " she gestures as if all that is beneath contempt, "I have to think about it." Something in the easy way she is sitting by the table gives me the feeling she is there to stay. But she isn't.

"Thas gud," she says, pours the last of the brandy in her tea, downs it, straightens her cloak, puts on her hat, gives me a satisfied closemouthed grin, and leaves.

I sit looking stupidly at the dark wedge between the door and the jamb before I shake myself and dash out on the porch to pull the light on. There is no sound, she is nowhere to be seen. Listening to be sure she is not stumbling around in the dark I turn the bulb off again and go inside. This is no time for silly games.

I think of the electrocardiac arrhythmias section of the text that must be memorized, an assessment on inter-relational capabilities of the normal family unit, and a paper on the handling of secondary inertia in postpartal depressional patients, with a view to their functionally productive return . . . All due tomorrow.

And of course, the Denvers. I could pretend I've got Michael here giving me his views on being a normal happy three year old. I could maybe spin a Denver out around Harlin's toe. No time to lose! I slap two slices of bread around a hunk of cheese, fill the kettle with strong tea and start to work.

Having pulled the curtain on the moon I crank out more than I thought possible and at ten minutes to ten when I stop for a breather there is clean copy on the sociology assessment lying to my right, three typewritten pages on postpartal inertia on the bookshelf, an outline of trigger words highlighting the main arrhythmic properties of damaged heart muscle, and one Denver on Michael, who for purposes of confidentiality I call Bobbi.

Rummaging at the back of the bottom desk drawer for a blank DD form, my fingers brush a small dry package. Breaking the string, laying it before me, I unfold the brown grocery paper. Daffy-down Dilly, I had forgotten!

Four inch bumble bee, tumbled disheveled tendril rootlets nestling like sea lettuce in my palm. Trillium, Three-Leaved Nightshade, Bethroot. I'd dug her from the dark patch between the tamarack and the monastery wall the year my acceptance into the community was postponed the second time. I figured, if I had to leave I'd take a small portion of enclosure with me. Afterwards I found out she was on the endangered species list in New York State.

Her red-haired sisters can be a bit pungent. Ill Scented Wake-Robins they're called, or more crudely, Stinking Benjamins. But Truelove or Birthroot, appearing early in March in her white gown, never smelled anything but beautiful to me. She was removed from the National Formulary in 1949, her astringent properties effectively lab-copied.

The rhizome, its tiny corn—like a single eye—rests lightly in my palm. Compact little powerhouse, wild lover of dark canopies. Be brave it seems to say, go! join them, and take me with you.

CHAPTER 12

There is a motorized wind roaring through the hills, winnowing the bare trees, whipping the evergreens; I think I hear chanting but as I strain after it the hint is blown and tumbled, bent and cracked against wood. Once I make it to the ridge top I wrap my hand about the Trillium tucked deep in my coat pocket, in the other pocket I'm carrying the candle Iah told me to bring although what on earth I'll do with a candle on a night like this I do not know.

The moon is full. I imagine she cackles at the tumult. Unable to hear I feel vulnerable, an involuntary shiver shakes me. Chanting rises and falls from the hollow on the springboard of the wind, a dozen or so lights form a circle, there is no bonfire.

"Lady of the winds . . . Lady of the tides . . . Mother Diana, bless us your assembled children. Queen of the moon . . . Queen of the stars . . . Queen of earth . . .

"Lady of the winds . . . Lady of the tides . . ." the chanting increases in volume as I descend the slope, using the tree trunks to slow my progress.

Dressed in light colored robes eighteen or nineteen women and men walk to a dark preappointed center. Holding hands, they raise their arms, directing a great sigh through the top of their pyramid to the night sky, then, dropping their arms, back up. Compressing and expanding the circle they chant the flower's leaping for the moon.

The rhythmic cadence of the chant is flute magic to the inner light. Standing on the level earth just outside the circle, I am caught up in the chant as the golden one in her looping spiraling pattern burns her way up my spine.

A figure leaves the center of the circle and approaches, two people breaking handclasp to allow her to pass. "May the Lady bless your vision and your life!" My two hands are clasped in rough warm ones and a look as shimmering as mercury or dew on cabbage leaves holds my gaze. The eyes laugh, "we were ineffectual in whistling down the wind tonight, I am Calamus."

She takes a step back and looks at me, smiling a secret smile, and nods her head decisively, "we do not close the circle to the moon. Did you bring a candle?"

The hands part as we walk to the center where many candles are stuck upright in a large basin full of sand. Finding space among the grains for mine, I secure it. I turn and the circle closes upon us, a great tent of arms rising above, closing out the world to all but the disc of silver. Gold rushes up my spine to the loaf of moon bread.

I burn while the wave of humanity recedes and when they return to compress the center again I raise my arms. After the next compression, hands grab mine and I am pulled to the circumference as part of the human circle.

I know mystics down through recorded history have said we were one. I believe them, intellectually. But it was never a knowing as it suddenly is there at that moment. There, while the rippling inner light shoots off its fireworks display, I know it. It makes all the difference.

Calamus, standing at the center, has given a sign with the pointed object she carries. All chanting stops, a low hum, similar to the droning of a quiet contented hive replaces it.

Long hair no longer flails about. Robes hang straight down without rippling, the wind has dropped. The humming does not increase as much as deepen, become guttural. The hive is stirring. Stretching outward as far as we can, taking care not to step on the flashlights that mark the outer circle, a sudden coordinated whoosh of sound leaves the circumference imploding inward.

The candles on the altar light as if passed over by an invisible hand, they flash! A deep sigh escapes those assembled. Then, everyone is laughing, hugging, kissing, pounding their neighbor on the back. I am hugged, kissed and passed on to the next. A strong thrust against my back starts me coughing. Two gentle hands right me, "sorry!" I am handed on.

Calamus calls from a cluster of four or five people, someone walks up to a crate, leaves something and walks away. "A fine Esbat, don't you think, a fine Esbat!"

"Yes, yes," again, I agree. For a silent moment I watch the candles in the cast iron pot burning . . . all of them, including mine, burning. A woman on my left turns to me, "if you have anything that is precious to you this is the time to release it. But if you have nothing," she makes haste to add, "the Lady will understand."

Behind me I see the man with the gentle paws look at a worn, well-washed ribbon in his hand that might once have been red. Taking a last look he walks stolidly forward, laying it gently on the wood. Appreciative of privacy, people make their way forward one by one.

Thoughts rush through me. A celebration? A coming into the open of deep communion? I mean, where have I experienced such kinship? In the monastery?

Yes . . . but seldom as here tonight. I have to be honest with myself. But, I have nothing to give. I came without even a flashlight. I had a candle, and my precious Bethroot, my cloister away from home. My fingers, holding the supple tendrils, squeeze down.

For a long time I stand hunched weighing what looks like a great sacrifice against the laws of the unconscious as I know them. A gift on one level has to be reciprocated on another; as in this case, a tangible material form is expected as acknowledgement of what I know on the elusive plane.

As I take the warm rhizome from my pocket and lay it next to the once-red ribbon I hear Calamus' voice: "For I am the gracious Goddess who giveth the gift of joy unto the heart of woman and man. Upon Earth I give peace, and freedom and reunion with those who have gone before, nor do I demand sacrifice for behold, I am the Mother of all living and my love is poured out upon the Earth."

"It works." Following the five women into the house, I encounter the crazy scientist rendition of their stove and am dumbfounded at the extensiveness of its twists and turns.

"Well, as long as it works," I laugh. It is almost one-thirty when the group disbands from the clearing and these five women invite me in for a drink, or talk. Too keyed up to go home and sleep, I accept.

Seuell Connor, the black woman I met with her little girl at the Thriftway some months ago is one of the five. I don't see her little girl, but I caught Seuell's brilliant smile from across the circle early on.

Settled on a big round pillow under overhanging duct work I look around while Iah and Calamus futz over the number of cinnamon pods to add to the remaining mulled wine. Seuell disappears into a back room. Thalak feeds two black cats. And Morelle rummages in a bread box, "Are you hungry? crackers?"

"No, I don't think so, I don't feel hungry, I feel just fine!"

"Well, that doesn't mean you don't care for wine, here," Calamus' long stride has covered the distance from the kitchen in two leaps and she places the warm mug in my hand. Iah, putting the kettle on the flat stone before the stove flops down beside me, "So glad ya cum back fer a spell!"

"Don't talk until I get there!" Seuell shouts from the rear.

"And she's always late," Thalak mutters, closing up the cat food and joining us on the floor. The oldest, she is a round little woman no taller than five foot two, with blue eyes and very long white hair, which she wears coiled about her head like a turban. Fine lozenges of silver flicker in her ears as she talks. She is sixty-seven.

Seuell prances into the room, drops a sleeping bag between the wall and our backs, throws herself prone, wraps her arms about the bag and, "oooh la la . . . ooooh la la, waren't tha a fine nigh! Ohh sisters! we got ourselves one fine nigh!" her eyes roll heavenward in the stark blackness of her face.

Her roly, custard Georgian tones make me laugh. She pokes a finger at me in mock indignation, a sly tint of challenge in her gaze. "She dare to laugh, she dare to laugh at a Witch!" Didn't know that day you was fraternizing with a Witch, did you!?" The dare is quite open now. A crazed cackle comes from deep within her throat. Carried away by her own theatrics she pounds and hugs the bag until it's a ball. Curling her arms and legs around it she becomes a beetle rolling her dung.

"She snapped again?" Morelle is looking at her in bemused affection from the door. Standing backlit like that, her mass of blond, almost white hair stands around her head like a halo.

"Now we all gather, I wan ta hear wha ye think of Witch," Iah's hand touches mine. "No need for her to tell us what she thinks about Esbat celebrations." There is a murmur of assent, "yes, tell us how you feel about Witch."

I look around me. I don't know these women very well, I hesitate. They wait patiently. "I, I get a sick feeling in my stomach when I hear the word," I know I look sheepish but everyone is nodding assent. A low "aha" travels around the room.

"I am what men call Witch," Calamus is speaking . . . " this means one who has some knowledge of medicine, of herbs, of simples and magic, and who holds a key to some of the mysteries that lie hid in nature." She sighs.

Seuell unfolds from her beetle position. "Woman's got powa. That powa gotta cum from sompin bad. Us bad . . . real baad . . . baa . . . baa . . . baaaaa," Iah kicks her gently in the middle of a particularly long baaaa. I am fascinated by the changing coloration of her speech. From sweet-custard south to southern Bronx vodoo to middle-class ASP, she wears accents like bargain basement hats from Filene's, dropping them, moving on.

"I like ta tell ye how I learn I be Witch," Iah leans forward. "I being raped. He go ta sit down on the char, take off is boots? I will tha char ta tha end of tha room. It not thar when he sit."

"Mad? Goddess, he be real mad! I canna git away. Take tha, tha, tha, you Witch, he say." Wonderment floods her face remembering, "I no feel a thin, I lie there wonderin at tha char! I practice, I watch wha I kin do," she looks deep into her mug. "He righ! I owe im. I pay im back 'n' he leave me alone then."

"When evil comes, turn it around and make it work for you."

"Righ!"

"I was always sensitive to vibes," Calamus is talking, "Never thought much of it, many people, especially women, are sensitive to the energy given off by others. They have had to be. But, one day I had the distinct impression my mind was taking up more space. Sounds crazy? It was a funny opening-out sensation, as if consciousness were being rolled out like pie dough on top of a lot of other pie dough. I was able to see and hear things from a distance. Knew what was going to happen. Found a book on ESP, but it wasn't much help."

"Written work is a motley assortment of truth, semi-truth, and out-and-out make believe."

Calamus nods in agreement at Thalak's statement. "I did find something on precognition and the psychic clairvoyant power, knew it was right the minute I read it!" She looks at Iah, "it's been practice for me too. If I hadn't found this bunch," she smiles affectionately, "I'd probably be in the loony bin.

"I knew," her eyes rest on mine, "a woman was enrolling in Saddleback who carried a light energy that was often a confusion. She was going to live in the hill house. For thousands of years the house on poles has stood for the home of an ancestral spirit, one who could be consulted for guidance."

"Do you know that at times you stand out like a torch?" I shake my head in embarrassment. "You don't have any say in how it flows?"

"Not really. Sometimes I can stop it. It's been a recent occurrence for me to retain consciousness when it fills my head."

Everyone is pensive. Seuell, sitting in modified lotus, looks like a brown Buddha. Thalak strokes a cat's ears. Fine strands of Morelle's hair, caught in invisible warm air currents, float web-like around her still head.

When she speaks this web vibrates gently, "I feel energy fields. What I feel tells me as much, if not more, than my five senses." She catches a gossamer filament from between her eyes, carries it back across her head and pats it in place.

Thalak is looking intently at her. "Remember, it's as much a 'sense' as the more familiar ones, a psychic sense to be sure, different dimension."

Morelle smiles, "you're right, I know, it's just that it's still so new to me . . . " She looks across to me, "I must be absolutely still, and I must have something connected to the person or place I am tuning in on; I need it here within my two hands," she rubs her palms together, "some little material object they've been close to.

"No change in consciousness like Cal, it's more of an activation of sorts on a body level. A whirlpool starts here, just below my diaphragm and glows like brandy, then, I begin to receive impressions, sometimes very confusing impressions." Her tone changes and she sits up and puts her shoulders back, "I'm no longer afraid. And I have started meditating . . . it helps a lot, it grounds me."

"Seuell will not tell you herself," Calamus says, as the brown Buddha buries her head, "but she's quite a healer. She may look like a voodoo priestess, but as an ex-CNM she's definitely a Witch!" Hey, hey! the chorus agrees.

"You don't have a coven?"

"Aha-ha! you do know something about the craft!"

"Not much, really," I laugh, "in fact very little. I happened to come across a few books on matriarchal religion this past Christmas. I was completely caught up in thinking through . . . " my voice is suddenly far away . . . "the very real psychic change that takes place when I shift from an infinite God-being to the infinite as Goddess. I mean, I suddenly see all sorts of repercussions, within!"

My voice has become animated, both cats are looking at me from Thalak's lap, their ears tipped, their eyes wide and numinous. I rein in my excitement, "I, I've been thinking about the difference it would make in my life."

Everyone is silent. Six women seemingly dropped in our delirium from the moon. "We have what we call a group," Seuell says, "it's more open than a coven. There is a Dianic coven, a feminist coven about twenty miles from here."

"You mean there are others around?"

"Well! not like us!" Seuell's eyes roll in mock pretension, "but oh Goddess yes! quite a few, there's rebels in these here hills."

Morelle intersperses, "They mainly call themselves

pagans; sense of sickness at the stomach is quite common at the sound of the word Witch. We have books you could read . . . Three years ago . . . Tell her about" . . . suddenly everyone is talking at once.

At a lull in the conversation I lean in Seuell's direction. She is lying on her side atop the opened sleeping bag cradling her tight mass of dreadlocks. "You look tired." The nod and smile are weary-satisfied.

"It's been busy . . . I've got three visits to make this morning." She shakes her head over unknown vagaries, the stone sculpture of her hair unmoving.

"How is your little girl, how is Burnet?" I know as soon as I've said it that it is the wrong thing to say. I see the change in her. I feel the sudden full attention of the other women.

Seuell's eyes close. The indrawn breath seems to go on forever. The exhalation, when it comes, is forced through her teeth. She lies still for thirty seconds, then, sitting up, swivelling on the base of her spine, she slides her legs into modified lotus and faces me.

"My daughter does not choose to live with her mother. She wants to live in the city with her grandmother." Calamus reaches an arm toward her which Seuell, shaking her head, wards off with a raised palm. "It's true. It's true." The voice is low, "my daughter wants her TV. She wants to shop at the malls. There are no ballet classes where her mother lives. Her mother has no money, anyway, and couldn't send her to dance even if there were such things in the hills. My daughter is TV-American. And it's my fault." The voice breaks, "my own damn fault." Calamus jumps up to hold her while the black woman sobs.

"It would be difficult for her here, you know that, Sue."

"Not impossible . . . we could do it," the words are muffled against Cal's neck.

"It's different with you . . . kids can be cruel . . ." She looks at us with sad eyes over Seuell's bent head.

The birds are making soft, chittery wakeup sounds as I let myself in the cabin. And the wind-packed snow above the plank door falls on my head. The stove is cold. A shake on the mushroom-shaped handle clears the grates of ash. Opening the damper wide, I crumble paper and build a tepee of kindling over it, strike a match and add three medium-sized logs.

It flares, and once it settles to feed I scatter coal and close the door. Fire was kept by woman in her fingernails, in her genitals, at the end of her digging stick . . .

Everyone has her Patmos. She is free to go or not to go onto that terrifying promontory of thought from which darkness is perceived. If she does not go she remains in ordinary consciousness, in ordinary virtue, in ordinary faith or doubt. It is just as well. For ordinary peace it is obviously better. If she goes on that peak she is caught. The profound waves of the marvelous have appeared to her. No one sees that ocean with impunity . . . a certain quantity of her will belong to darkness as the boundless enters into her life. In this twilight, enough of her former life will be distinguished in order to seize the two ends of dark thread to tie her soul together again. Victor Hugo said.

I forgot to ask who Silesia is.

At nine a.m., I am culturing a feverish six year old's strep throat. At ten-thirty, beginning to feel the strain of continuous wakefulness, I have an urge to put my head down on the examining table.

I am attempting a Denver Developmental on a three year old sitting atop her mother's knee. Simple, really, I mean, it's just a series of questions and responses. The rigid mass of Shirley Temple curls, the stormy brown eyes—not buying it—she sets her chin and clenches her teeth.

"She backward?" The mother shifts pleading brown eyes my way then the two of us watch Leanne as she rolls up her hem, smoothes it out, rolls up her hem, smoothes it out . . . I am mesmerized by the motion. "She backward isn she?"

"No!" I shake myself. Having watched my brothers and sisters worry over lazy eyes, bowed legs, toed-in syndromes, possible spinal curvatures and crooked teeth I cringe, I cannot stand to see these women struggle with any more guilt. We are told to say it's a test of developmental growth, which means absolutely nothing. Of course they read it as a test of normalcy.

I want to say the test is a training tool for us students in assessing guidelines, but parents wouldn't sit very long in these stifling cubicles for that.

"She's a normal toddler, wary of strangers."

"You sure?"

"Yes!" and as I say this I am thinking of Miss Privis, who says we must get these children into the system early if they are going to be healthy adults. "Their

health depends," she says, "on frequent, early exams."
I thought "Pater familias" was on the wane!

"Miss Mark, your notes are improving but, they're quite terse." We are sitting after a long clinic going over my charts and Miss Privis has been mentioning that my coverage leaves something to be desired. "See, here is a note written by," she mentions one of my classmates, "do you see how she carries the essentially relevant facts of the medical history through the extended history outline . . ."

"Easy to read, isn't it? I know the patient's reason for being here, it is mentioned at the beginning of the diagnostics, but a summary is in order." She looks up to see if I am following. "Make sure infectious diseases are included in this summary . . . previous hospitalizations . . . surgery . . . injuries, I see you covered this nicely. And now, the present illness, you have two sentences." She purses her mouth. "I was thinking more in line of two paragraphs."

"Document, Miss Marks! document! You know how important charts are, you never know when one may be called up. But, don't be discouraged," she gives me a diked little smile, "your charting is getting better!"

CHAPTER 13

Hail is pelting from a low grey ceiling making all level surfaces unnavigable as I climb the hill to Wednesday Cottage for lunch. There is a smell of chicken and tuna in the air. Ellen and Lisa in the living room munching on sandwiches, look up briefly from their reading and nod, mouths full.

Linda and Judy, two seniors, are in the kitchen just finishing up. They'll be out of my way in a minute, they say. "It's OK." I smile and opening the big old refrigerator door reach my hand to the back left corner where I left my chicken soup. It's not there. "Where's my soup!" My voice is a child's voice, petulant with disappointment.

"Probably turned bad and someone threw it out," Linda does not meet my eyes.

"Ta-ta," Judy says, throwing her bowl upside down on the drain board before following Linda out of the kitchen.

I stand stupidly looking at the empty space that held my lunch. "Listen, I've got some tuna made up and a fresh loaf of bread . . . " Lisa is at my elbow.

"I left bread . . . " my voice trails off.

"It may not be here."

"You sure you have enough?" In answer, she reaches to the lowest shelf and retrieves a carton with her name on it.

She is pouring boiling water from the kettle onto her already soggy tea bag. "Listen, I, I don't think I'm going to be able to copy those study guides any more for you." Her brown eyes are troubled as they search my face, "I feel badly about it but I just don't have time . . . there isn't enough time . . . !"

"Oh, listen, it's alright. Don't worry about it, I'll manage. I understand. Everyone is swamped!"

"Are you sure?"

My mouth full of tuna sandwich, I nod, making an indecipherable grunt. Lisa gives me a weak grin.

Afterwards, sitting alone in the living room looking out into the smog from the coal fires in the town below, I wonder about those old exams and the best way to get hold of them. It's very difficult if you don't live in the dorms, but it can't be impossible. I don't blame Lisa, it was her idea to get them to me in the first place. I didn't know anything about them until she told me they were being circulated around the hill.

Descending hospital hill, heeling into dirt, jagged rock, upended slab, anything obstinate, I arrive taut but whole at the back door of the hospital.

"Ninety-nine, ninety-nine, ninety-nine . . . " he is nervous and I cannot feel the vibration. "Can you deepen your voice, Mr Cullen?"

"Ninety-nine," the pitch descends. Two flushed areas on his cheekbones breaking the grey pallor of his face, a small dark man sits shirtless on the end of the examining table. The flat palm of my hand is against his chest.

Right infraclavicular fossa, then the left one . . . "ninety-nine," I make my way down the chest wall by way of the vocal fremitus against my palm.

All the vibrations that speech sets up in the bronchial air column are conducted to the chest wall. "You're doing very well, Mr. Cullen," I say, he sits a little taller. "I need to go over this side again," I gesture to his left, was it the seventh or the eighth interspace? I've lost count.

Beginning at the clavicle I make my way down the

barrel-shaped chest wall. There! at the eighth interspace, considered a false rib . . . up through the seventh true rib . . . increased density associated with? inflammation? pneumonia? lung abscess?

"Mr. Cullen, we're going to need fresh X-rays."

"Been avin em ever since they let me off at the mine." He coughs a sewage-slop sound. Is it safe to say that every other male of working age has some degree of black lung?

I need someone to check my percussion and auscultation and can't find Mrs. Kane. Dr. S. is getting a drink at the water fountain.

In quick sure movements he places his stethoscope against the man's chest wall . . . anterior, posterior, upper, lower . . . he ascultates briefly, "X-ray," he says.

"What do you think about my findings?"

He shrugs good naturedly, "you're probably right, but I always say, why waste time? X-ray," he smiles and is gone.

The idea I have of the end of the world, the one where the little man pushes the broom along endless, deserted, antiseptically-smelling corridors, always has a large no-nonsense clock on the wall. Sometimes the maintenance man smiles and bobs as I pass, but the corridor is always a composite of all the hospital wards and all the late night clinics I've ever worked.

In the parking lot, snow packs underfoot like amalgam in a tooth. Fine hensfoot frost tracings cover the entire car. Cleaning the windshield. Climbing in thinking with satisfaction of the paper work finished, I turn the key.

The flywheel . . . like the worlds . . . revolves in a vacant lot. No ignition. No response. The car will not start. How will I get home? Where will I sleep? Keep calm! a little voice says, stop scattering negative vibes on this poor cold engine!

Breathing and exhaling deeply I watch smudge build up on the inner glass. Again I turn the key, but all the forced calm in the world does not spark ignition. Eventually the uselessness of running down the battery seeps through to me.

The only one I can find in all the administrative/classroom complex is a secretary to the dean closing up her office. She tells me she cannot recommend anyone in town as relations have been strained with the local garages. But she does allow me to use the phone.

Sitting on a stool by her desk, as she goes off to do some last minute chore, I call garages, tows and car mechanics. Five calls later, a man says, "I'm busy," but he does not follow this with a mighty groan, nor "absolutely no way!" nor, "ugh-ugh!"

He hesitates as if looking over his shoulder at chores still to be done, "It may be a half hour before I get there," he says.

"Blue Ford Pinto with New York plates," relief surges through me, "I'll be waiting by the car in the lot. Thank you!"

I spend the next ten minutes holding up the wall by the rear door watching the vent on the kitchen extension belch hot steam; I imagine minute crystals tinkling onto frozen ground. But the enforced inactivity finally gets to me, if I don't move, I'll lie down right there in the hall and sleep.

Back out into the cold I go to clear the frost from all the windows. Offhandedly, as I am scraping the inner windshield, I turn the key again.

She coughs! she sputters! she starts! Poetry, sheer poetry! I sit there for a few minutes revelling in the sound of the stalwart motor. Then, remembering the mechanic, I put her in gear and chug off to find Caruthers Garage at the corner of Pikaly and Pine.

Both pumps are busy. A Chevy Blazer is parked before one of the garage doors, and a battered green pickup, pulled horizontal with the windows of the adjoining shop, has its motor running.

Pulling alongside the Blazer I get out but do not shut off the engine. The man pumping gas, watching me as I start to walk toward him, ducks quickly behind a truck. The body-language is all too obvious, I change direction and walk around the tailgate of the pickup, open the door and enter the low ceiling'd smokey room.

Three middle aged men are joking good naturedly just inside the door. Each one of them takes a step back; a watchful expression falls over three identical faces. Two men sipping coffee, stop and eye me motionless over the plastic rims. An old man with a crooked back busys avoiding my eyes by counting oil tins.

One wall of the room opens into the large double bay of the garage, my eyes search around the truck up on the far lift and as I do a dolly rolls out from under the Jeep in the foreground. The young man sitting up on it stares at me. As I am about to speak to him a man comes out of a corner room. He is wiping black hands on a rag, I meet his eyes.

"Called twenty minutes or so ago, had a stalled car.

Spoke to someone who was kind enough to say he would come and check it for me." His eyes are guarded, he wipes his hand slowly and thoroughly on the cloth.

I try again, "I spoke to someone here, I just wanted to let him know that the car started, and I'll, I'll be fine, don't want him making a trip for nothing." Neither the man nor the boy sitting upright on the dolly make any sound or motion that would indicate they have heard.

Strange! At least I tried. Shifting weight, turning to leave, the deep baritone catches me essentially airborne, "You spoke to me."

My gaze swings away to the far wall of the garage where a man, who has crawled out from under the truck, is straightening his shoulders; his back to me, there is a weariness in the line of spine, the dishevelled mop of grey hair.

I wait while he finishes, something in that back holding me. When he turns he doesn't move wearily, he steps around the Jeep and crosses the floor as if he owns it. Circling the cash register, he hooks a finger on a jacket, strides around me without glancing my way, crosses to the door which he props open with a foot while he shrugs wide, spare shoulders into the denim.

Once the jacket is on he meets my glance. Looking for one long moment he sees whatever it is he sees through those calm, grey eyes. When he gestures me unblinking to the door, it is with the barest, silent nudge of his head. Holding it open, he waits while I pass and follows me to the car.

For ten minutes he pokes wordlessly around the motor: he drains the radiator, adds resealant, disconnects battery leads, wipes and sandpapers. Drawing a line of hose from a low partition in the door he fills the battery, which is almost empty.

He is holding the hose inside the radiator looking at me quietly, "Helps to put water in a car when ya want it to run for you." His eyes are the solitary grey of the wolf, the fox, the coyote encountering something two-legged on their own turf. The essentiality of such placement in being hits me in the chest. I can't find anything to say.

"Keep ya busy over there?" I smile weakly. "Long way from home." I nod and pull my eyes away from his. "I was in New York once," he withdraws the hose from the radiator and turns the nozzle.

"How did you like it?" my voice sounds strange to me.

The square jaw with the day-old stubble feigns whimsy, "S'OK I guess, to visit."

"There are sections of upstate New York that you would like, not quite as corrugated as here," I look over his shoulder at the darkened hills, "but very beautiful."

"You don't live in the city?" he is leaning easy against the roof of the Pinto as if he hasn't a thing in the world to do, the hose with its spray shut off dangling in his hand. I realize he is waiting for my answer.

"No." I can't think of anything to say. I feel the man's lean strength. No wobble here. A bit over six foot, early fifties. Standing there looking silently in his eyes I feel like I'm being pulled down a well. He breaks his gaze to look down at the toe of his boot and when he raises his head there is a quizzical lift to his left brow.

"How much do I owe you?" The shaggy grey shakes definitely from side to side. "But!"

The look is questioning, appraising and teasing all rolled into one. The voice laconic. "We all need water." A flush courses to my forehead. Winning over some urge to say more, he steps back. In the rear view mirror I see him stand in that one spot watching while I drive away. And the fox could dance around Brer Rabbit if he chose!

The supermarket on the outskirts of town is enjoying its dinnertime lull. I look for something for supper, a miasma called fatigue flowing out parodying my movements; I can't decide between meat, chicken or eggs . . . something high in protein . . . easy to fix I am thinking, as turning a corner, I run into another shopper.

Eyes down arguing the pros and cons of eggs I shuffle to one side as the feet opposite do the same, immediately I try the other way, the feet follow. We could do this all night, I look up chuckling, into Thalak's smiling face. "Yer mind was far away."

"On food," I say smiling wearily.

"Don't you keep anything ready for these late nights?" she looks concerned.

"My larder was exhausted."

"That's not the only thing that be exhausted," she looks at my basket, "have you the things you need?" When I nod she puts a hand purposefully next to mine on the cart and starts steering it in the direction of the checkout girl, "You're coming home with me!"

"Thalak! I can't!" I try to breathe her name the way Calamus does, with the emphasis on 'Tha' as in stay, looping the L after it and finishing with only a brief touching down of the 'ak' at the rear of the palate.

"Yes, you can!"

"I'm so tired, Thalak, I just want to go home, eat something and sleep, sleep, sleep!"

"I'm on the way. You follow me, you eat, and then you go on up to 'owl' and sleep. Follow me," her lilting voice is determined, "watch carefully before the climb from the valley, I'll be taking off on a westward spur." I watch as she climbs into a battered tan Toyota.

Starting the car, I marvel at how full of surprises people can be. Last night, was it only last night? Thalak kept demurely to the background, watching with pleasure the ongoing spirited conversation, but rarely joining in; she was the Kleinmaster from German art history. Tonight, the little skilled master who doesn't draw attention to herself is suddenly a moving force to be reckoned with.

Oh why fight it! it's been a long day. How can an hour hurt? Watching her wheel out of the supermarket lot I shift quickly and step on the gas. I had no idea she lived up "Owl."

She drives the one lane from the river like a daemon, spinning at the gravel pit, barreling along the flat, over the frozen ground and through the bulrushes; if it weren't for the cattails glowing and bobbing in the headlights I couldn't follow.

It is not a road, more a pair of ruts which I straddle. She is right though, it isn't very far. When she stops her car the headlights illumine a curved, shovelled path and a white door. A light goes on behind a tall thin window to the right of the door, thirty seconds later lights come on to the left.

"Make yourself at home, I'm going to ready our supper; have some wonderful pies!" Her head disappears. Kitchen sounds swallow up the last of the words. The room is large, warm and well-lit and has a long wall, opposite the door, of solid fieldstone; twenty-four feet, floor to ceiling, drywall construction, it gives the impression of great permanence and age.

In this wall, immediately opposite me, a fireplace opening is fat with stove. Black, belly proud, seven feet high, five feet wide, it surveys me. Plank floors, braided rugs . . . A round table before one large window holds a dented copper kettle, a kettle full of dried amber stalks; bent and winged, herbs or legendary rocs, they fly above the table.

The gentle but persistent nod, nod, nod of a blunt object against my leg says, "see me, see me! I'm down here, let's meet!" When I stoop, he sits back on black haunches, washes his face, and turns a regal feline gaze my way, quite ready for the auspicious event. I dare not insult such royalty with speech, I sit back on my haunches and will my greeting into his eyes. It is accepted.

He follows me to the south wall as I go to look over the stacks of books behind the reading chairs and floor lamps. *The Mothers* by Robert Briffault; *The Cult of the Black Virgin* by Ean Begg; *Excavations at Jerico* by Kenyon and *Goddess of Love* by Grigson . . . but I know some of these!—my eyes range over the haphazard piles—some of them I left back in the scriptorium inked with fresh Library of Congress numbers.

To the right of the random stacks a heavy oak bookcase draws me. Botany, principles of pharmacology, indigenous drugs of India, China, Mexico, Peru, Egypt. Traditional medicine, relationships of plant roots to the soil, seed capabilities in changing environments . . . all I ever wanted to know about herbs is sitting right here in this one bookcase.

I am examining a plate depicting a bright yellow rootstock about three-quarters of an inch thick; dozens of slender rootlets hang their veils from its underside; the top surface is marked with scars.

"Previous years of flowering . . . each scar a stalk. Here!" Thalak hands me a tall thin glass full of cherry-tinted liquid, "I make this myself."

I sip. "Mmnnn, it's good!"

"I'm going to make us a salad, you look like you could use a few sprouts. Ten minutes, give or take, we eat," she swivels on her feet and the loosened end of a braid arcs about and flops down the back of her neck. "Oh, you'd be interested in the contents of that room there," she gestures with her head at the wall of fieldstone.

"That's a door!?"

"What did you think it was?"

"A cupboard? for wood or coal?" I falter, I hadn't really thought too much about it, I just took for granted the stone wall was the outer wall of the house.

She points with her finger to her nose. "Light string hanging just about nose level, inside." Then she continues to the kitchen. As she goes I realize I haven't made half a gesture of help, what a dolt! I hesitate for a moment looking at the door, it is intriguing.

The planks, pegged together by three heavy crossbars at the rear, swing easily on metal pins sunk deep in stone. A rush of warm moist air greets me. In the illumination thrown over my shoulder I see the string and pull it. Four soft lights go on at once in the barn-like room.

I step inside, the heavy door closing silently behind me. Dirt. I scuff my boots, stirring up the softness. Dark peaked ceiling beams, from which hang the most amazing assortment of rumpled shapes. For one moment I think bats, and my body backs up involuntarily. You know how bats look in their sleep! the inner voice is chagrined. These are not bats!

The heat from the wall is very mellow. It seeps into the large cave-like room through the stone? through apertures? or mini grottos in the wall? Six caves group themselves around the area directly back of the stove. Some hold bulky burlap packages which lean helter-skelter. Drying? Two hold open-mouthed urns.

There is no way of knowing what is ahead on this journey, no means of predicting. I have visited cathedrals, toured famous shrines, spent hours in adoration before the Blessed Sacrament.

I have felt the light ascend within and known the numinous. Why am I kneeling then suddenly on dirt, under hundreds of hanging shapes—evidently roots drying—near a high stone wall? Why indeed am I crying?!

For what we've lost. I am sobbing out my heart on the dirt, drops of liquid pocking the earth around my knees, with the answer clairaudient within me. For what we've lost. For what we have not found. For what we find and do not recognize.

CHAPTER 14

"**Child! what on earth!**" she settles on the dirt behind me and puts her arms about my shoulders. I don't know where it all comes from. Great sobs tear through my belly and lungs, tears splatter the dirt I crouch on. Some time passes. I feel the gentle rock, rock, rock and hear the soft inch of cloth being dragged back and forth across the ground. My head is sheer to bursting. Sniff . . . "I love this room, Thalak. I," sniff, "love this room."

"That's good," her voice is wry, "it doesn't usually have this effect on people. Not that I let many in here. But no one as yet has muddied the dirt, look! just look," she gestures about us.

Avenues of flow shooting off the saturated twill of my jacket have joined a zig-zag meander, a tiny mudflow oozes into the opening of my glove. I laugh. A laugh that sounds like a choked cough.

"Well, that's better!"

"He believed in a transcendent God," her eyes are far away as she places the empty stoneware one atop the other, "all over the world I listened to him preach a kind of infinity you worship, emulate, placate . . . but do not touch."

Her voice softens, "he loved his God, we had a good life together. When he died . . . well," she is silent. "It took awhile, but I finally admitted to myself that my God was incarnate, a modus operandi, if you will, a metamorphosing, coursing energy."

"Imagine finding this out after fifty! Imagine my surprise," she points to the book-strewn end of the room, "me thinking I was discovering something new all on my lonesome, to find that a lot of others thought that way too."

"I was surprised again when my changing flow

wouldn't adhere to a one-sided gender; God-the-father didn't fit into what I found at all," Thalak's hands go up to her braids and her mouth curves up in a childlike grin. "I thought I was so smart and there it was written. The books kept coming my way. But, I side with the Buddha," her eyes twinkle, "do not believe something because the written statement of some old sage is produced.

"It has to be in the heart, love is the law. And it harm no one do what thou will. All comes from the Lady . . . our allegiance is to the infinite one manifesting within."

"Some strange things have been happening to me . . ."

She gives me a piercing look, "You've had experience of a brand of energy that most call strange. Are you afraid of it?"

"No. But, I've lived with it for a long time."

"Teressa, we haven't even begun to tap our psychic energies, we're like children oohing and aahing over what we do not know, making up ghost stories about darkly, mysterious things to titillate our jaded nerve endings. Because we do not have the courage, nor the purity of life, to approach the next room in the house." She laughs a little laugh, "it will take time but it will come about. It will come about."

"The other night," she glances across the table affectionately, "I could see the fire shooting from your head quite clearly, the soma, the moon luster."

"I'm afraid I'm a very ineffectual vessel . . . There's more. In some way, there's more."

"You're proud that you're not a very effectual vessel, aren't you?"

I am startled. For a few minutes she sits and looks at me while I struggle to define my feelings to myself.

She's right. I guard the sense of inadequacy or sinfulness as if it were gold. Partly, it lets me off the hook, I can only do so much . . . after all?! Partly, it's a sense that any ultimate I might devise is going to fall far short of the mark; I do not trust my confused grasp of purity. A gift, then? A grace?

"I watch the conflicting emotions fly over your face. Wonderful!" she is laughing. "Let me recite something for you: 'Thou are luster in the moon, and radiance in the sun, intelligence in woman and man, force in the wind, taste in water and heat in fire. Without thee, O Goddess, the whole universe would be devoid of substance. All, O Mother, exists only by thy command!"

"That's beautiful!"

"From the Panchastavi," she has risen with a stack of dishes and I get up quickly to take them from her. "Albert Einstein once said that the attempt to combine wisdom and power has only rarely been successful, and then only for a short time.

"We're joining them, you know," her voice lowers, "with the Mother's help we will take responsibility for the powers springing from within."

Insomnia from inability to forget? Overtired is too simple a word for what I experience pacing the loft at 2 a.m., watching the clock face with panic; I must be up at 5!

I acted dangerously (for a nun) back at the garage. I forgot what that type of surcharge feels like. An ass, an unprepared complacent ass! If I can't monitor my instincts any better than that then I should wear the habit; put the onus on the other person to act with restraint and decorum.

And my emotionality at Thalak's? Well, I can accept that more easily, what with the stress and strain. The intensity of work . . . it makes sense in a place like this to cry once in awhile. They say some cry all the way through the program.

You were not crying about the program, you were crying over what you've found. It isn't in the right place, it doesn't conform to speculation.

I'm afraid and confused. What am I questioning? Why the awful sense of foreboding? I recall a young child who was going to be a priest. It's impossible, only men are ordained, Sister said. How preoccupied I then became with the humongous, red velvet fastened by its shiny brass end-pins to the marble, separating the sanctuary from the rest of the church. I belonged up there. Sister was wrong. If not Sister, then, someone . . .

A few years passed before I saw my chance to put a leg over the barrier. Walk with trepidation up the broad marble steps. Place my palm on the dazzling white linen cloth. Touch the tabernacle through its veil. Introibo ad altare Dei. I can still feel the warmth of the vigil light to the left of the curved gilt doors on my face. I was not struck down. The walls of the darkened, silent church were unmoved.

The sense of rightness I knew so many years ago is the same I knew on Thalak's floor. That can't be! It's cruel, a cruel trick at this time in my life.

A terrible agitation takes me. Look at me! It was unfair of Reverend Mother to send me off right now.

God knows, I need the support of the Community. I mean, struggling on professional and psychic levels with what I often do not understand . . . As a religious I have come close to the tabernacle, what more do I want?

I pull a cushion to the wall near the stovepipe and sit in modified lotus, Mother help!

Once in a rare while I have coaxed and S/he has risen immediately after having returned to her cave at the base of my spine, but seldom have I called as now and felt such immediate response.

The light that is indivisible bliss inches up my spinal column by insensible curves, wiping out the minutes' casual sequence. I welcome it, I never wished it more.

But something is different, something arrests the fire, it grows sluggish, slows, stops at the heart level. There it holds like a hovercraft. All my attention descends as a new astounding weight redistributes itself within my pelvis. Flashing open from closed fist to total expansion, the explosion of a thousand orgasms takes my breath away.

For one long moment ten thousand suns glow within my bony pelvis. Then, curling once more in upon himself the dragon goes back to sleep. Slowly, the amazing light that has been holding at chest level, waiting, descends, wraps herself about her brother, quiets, and stills.

If I suddenly discovered that I had three heads I couldn't be more surprised. They are two! They are two currents . . . all the years of believing the incredible spiralling fire was alone . . . !

Two! One etheric, of spirit substance, the other . . . much more earthy. A biological manifestation?

How does one describe such a manifestation? What I experienced was physical cellular change of unprecedented newness.

And yet, here I am no different than before. Well, hungry, yes, very hungry . . . And extremely horny. The soft tissue of my pelvis is wet and warm and in a definite state of tumescence. The kind you once associated with good foreplay, the inner watcher says.

Too much! I bolt from the loft, past the O'Keefe prints, around the hot stove, into the kitchen to raid the refrigerator. Half an hour later I climb back into bed and fall asleep.

152 **Yellow light in the face, bird song in the ear, I wake** in the sun-drenched room as easy as a babe. Behind the paper-thin ceiling birds are busy greeting, cajoling, menacing, preening, re-assuring; how many have found their way under the eaves? I am living in a bird house!

The clock says ten minutes to seven! Pickles and galoshes! There'll be no meditation this morning, and no time to review for the exam. I move with the unswerving rigor of a runaway train.

The car runs well. A twinge of regret, adagio-like, insinuates itself. It seems I had entertained a fleeting notion of baking someone a coffee cake. Well, it's too late now. But you can't be so ungrateful, so callous as to completely ignore a kindness. The inner dispute is on. The second voice exasperating in her pained meekness.

Without breaking, I turn the car left at the fork, and in less than three minutes am running across the supermarket parking lot, to return five minutes later with a box of fresh doughnuts in hand.

The pumps are not busy, there are no vehicles before the door. Pulling alongside the main entrance I leave the motor running and jump out clutching the box. There are three men in the room this morning. He is not one of them. They watch as I place the doughnuts beside the cash register, turn, and fly from the place.

The motion of relief has a fluid formula all its own. An easy glide, five minutes later having parked in the lot, I am hurrying through the snack room when the hospital utility elevator grinds to a halt.

"Miss Mark! Teressa? I wonder if I might have a word with you?" Mrs. Kane and I sit on the bench between soft drinks and Healthosnak. She is her usual flustered self; locking and unlocking her fingers; chairman-of-the-board-like she balances the stack of papers on her knees.

"Hummnn . . . humn . . . I've been checking grades." She falls silent. Balling up her right fist she squeezes it, then, releasing it, balls the left hand and squeezes it in sympathy.

When she finally speaks she shouts, "Did you know you have a 78 in Physio?!"

"Oh. Oh, I'm not worried about that." I shake my head in relief.

"You're not? You're not." She looks at me. I shake my head and watch her restless fingers quiet. "Well . . . if you're not worried . . . " I smile at her relief.

"I knew about it. I asked for a grade average last week . . . almost sorry it wasn't a 30 or 40 . . . would take some of the guesswork out of . . . " I stop, not entirely sure of what I am about to say.

The ice-making machine goes into action and we sit

listening to the chips fall. She doesn't make a move to rise and I glance at her staring at her, now motionless hands; a grey haired woman, pleasant face when it's in repose, she could be someone's grandmother.

"Mrs. Kane," my voice is soft, "what are you doing here?"

She doesn't answer at once and when she does it is with a voice I've never heard before, very steady and very calm. "I was lied to," her head is bowed, "just as you were lied to."

She turns and smiles wanly, "You see, I found myself with not much time left, and . . . the doctor I was working with, ahh, he was retiring, closing down his practice. I wanted to give something back, I, I felt I wanted to make some return for all the . . . "

Her eyes are on the two orderlies wrestling the stretcher from the elevator, but they do not see them, she sighs, "I read they needed clinicians. It seemed ideal, they promised me there would be no classroom teaching, I told them I was not up to that."

"When I arrived and saw the reality of the situation . . . I nearly left right then and there, I should have, oh I should have! They persuaded me to take a class, a month they said," she breathes deeply, "we were all deceived, you know, all deceived."

I've been holding my breath. Now I can breath again, "Mrs. Kane . . . "

"Tandy, I know the class calls me Tandy."

"Tandy, I need to find something positive to do." Now it's my hands that are restless with agitation. Something . . . anything . . . I was thinking of a class on the techniques of good gynecological examination." She does not move. "Those rubber models leave a lot to be desired." I find myself pleading.

Her voice is thin, high and threatened. "The school will not allow the students to do pelvic exams on each other!"

"A bit antiquarian, don't you think? Everywhere I've trained we've done exams on each other and been grateful for the experience."

"It's never been done here!" Her voice is dispirited.

"Yet we're in training to be midwives. If anyone needed to be able to do accurate pelvic exams, we do! I've taught self-help groups where the greenest recruit knows more about the axis of the uterus than any one of my classmates."

I feel better for having said it, but I really don't have much hope. When she turns and asks me what I would do I am surprised, but I hurry to explain. "I'd have a class on bi-manual and speculum exams . . . for anyone who wanted to come. Those who don't want to examine their classmates or be examined can come later, for of course we'll have a party! Yes, we'll have a celebration!" my voice is animated.

I can hear the smile in hers as she asks, "Am I invited?"

"Yes!"

Six of my class huddle outside the conference room after lunch. The list is up for in-service physicals and Erin and Ann are looking at me in sympathy, "You've got the hospital director, Tess! glad it's you and not us!"

The director, a middle-aged woman, is in the examining room promptly at 2 p.m. Her words put me at ease. "Thank God it is you," she says, "and not someone who doesn't know one end of a speculum from the other." The exam goes smoothly.

As she is leaving she turns at the door and gives me a searching look, "Teressa, I think I know what you're trying to do. These classes? You're trying to learn the material. Don't. Don't do it! you do not have time. Afterwards, when you are on your own, go into it in depth. For now just memorize and regurgitate it for the exams. Concentrate on passing the exams!" She smiles and is gone, the heavy door closing silently behind her.

For the heart in inner harmony and for which everything is one, no difference exists between this and that. I wish! No way am I able to claim the type of balance referred to by Monk Saihlen in twelfth century Japan. I don't want to leave the cabin for the hospital this morning and toy with the idea of calling in sick but, I know that I cannot, not on my first day on Medicine.

Horse tails of fine white outrun me as I drive. They careen wildly at the mine's box canyon and run up the sky, one by one. My thoughts play back Saturday's party and I smile to myself. When the three who did not come until it was time to eat arrived laden, they said we could be heard out past Dan and Tempi's.

When people left, calling goodbye over their shoulder on the way to the cars, I felt the cabin had been blessed.

New fallen snow and warm memories don't, I'm afraid, mask my stomach clenching, the fist within tightening with each mile, until, driving into the parking lot, the recoil is all too real. The flesh contests being here!

"Tess!" Allison's bright eyes look up from her mailbox, "it was wonderful being in a home again!" I smile my thanks, check my box which is empty, and start to walk down the corridor which fronts the doctor's conference room to the elevators at the other end.

I am ten feet from the conference room door when it opens, three doctors come out and a group of nurses flow around encircling them; the smell of fresh coffee reaches my nose.

Dr. D., his small figure trim and neat in his dark suit, his hair slicked seal-like to the sides of his head, looks up at my approach; his hand goes up as if stopping traffic, a nurse is caught with her mouth open in the middle of a word.

"We should have her present Grand Rounds," he turns to them, "do it on Self Help." He laughs, "hear it's the up and coming thing!" There is a smattering of reciprocal laughter from those around him.

I walk past without looking their way, pretending I have not heard, feeling gutted. Dapper little man with power of humiliation. I do not take the elevators, but walk the long way round and climb the front stairs.

As I come through the doors of the medical unit two older students look up. "Well!" one says, "I hear you had a party, and *we* weren't invited! I don't call that hospitable!" Her companion stares at me unblinking. I fix a non-committal smile on my face and whisper to my heart, "it will pass . . . it will pass."

"Tell 'em the forms must be filled out before they can be discharged, that'll stop all argument." Jumping from the cart she's been riding, stethoscope banging against a row of buttons on the crisp white pantsuit, our head nurse leaves. She is off to the emergency room. We look at each other and shrug; we have five pages of sociological data to collect this morning, and after lunch we are to do a complete exam. We move off in searching patterns.

The old gentleman in the bed by the door in 211 reminds me of Dan. I am reading his chart while he doses, the O of his mouth quivering like a bi-valve clam. The eyes open, focusing sleepily on me at the foot of the bed. "Doan av much time." It's a crotal sound, hollow, metallic and dull.

"Mr. Craig, my name is Miss Mark." Moving nearer I look into the pale, vague eyes. Ninetysix, progressive heart failure. "Doan wan em ta keep me." He sighs, and his fingers pluck at the covers. "No fuss. No fuss. Reddi. Been reddi." The eyes drift then close and he falls back to sleep.

Placing his chart with its NO ZERO CODE symbol gently back in its holder I tiptoe softly from the room.

A grey-haired corpulent woman is knitting in room 209, she looks up as I enter and smiles and is soon busy telling me why she is in the hospital for the third time this year.

From behind me a hand falls roughly on my arm. "I told you to leave her alone! I told em at the desk she was not to be bothered! All you people keep my mother from her rest, how is she going to get better if she can't get her rest!?" the woman in the nurses aide uniform is very angry.

"I'm so sorry, no one told me . . . " I back up, a mollified look appears on her face, but her shrill complaining follows me out the door.

Where to go next? There is no one in the hall, I am thinking eenie, meenie, minie, mo? and am looking over the doors, shuffling from foot to foot, when a lab technician backs a cart out of a room. Well, why not?

At the whoosh of the door closing behind, nine men dressed in Sunday black spin as one to face me. I've disrupted a congregation? With decided obstinacy the wall of faces attempt to stare me down. What are you doing here?! Who are you? You must deal with us! the faces say.

I look from one to the other seeking some human response, a chink in the united armor, a spokesman? a smiling elder? I have a feeling it will prove disastrous if I do not find someone in the silent battalion to address.

It is unsettling. I concentrate on meeting each pair of eyes and do not meet one flicker of warmth. I am facing a blank wall of guarded faces which I cannot penetrate. I stand very still, centering.

Without warning, the light breaks from her cave in my pelvis. She roars up my spine, awhirl and ablaze. And as she does, the dark separates, the sea parts. Unmenaced, at the center of this gathering, a woman's ironical, hypnotic gaze meets mine.

CHAPTER 15

Mount the dragon at the proper time and ride through the sky—advise the Chinese mystery schools; in other words, adjust, adjust to varying forces. Weighing the self manifest in the eyes before me. I watch it expand and grow luminous. Cat's eyes before the waxing moon.

One of the possible selves I've kept below my wall of opposites is enthroned like Pythia on her bed of vapors before me. Both hands are placed magical on her torso. I imagine I hear an escaping hiss, a savage will-o-wisp sound hanging sinuous in the air.

One can dispense with the civilities and socially prescribed forms at certain times. "We've met before?" Her voice is so resolute that the question is a mere nuance tacked on the end of a command.

"We've never met," I smile, "but we know each other."

The focus in the tiger eyes is intense; the amber, plunged into caves formed by root rot, smolders. It is my first meeting with the power of overlook, the ability of turning the gift of protection against your enemy, and the fact that it occurs in a sterile hospital room, one throng-full of ravens . . .

"Well, Innana, Ishtar, TellBrak . . . whoever you are . . . "

"My name is Kirke," she says in answer, bowing her head admirably. In the following pause there is an incalculable loosening of the guard, feet shuffle; I make note of it at the borders of my attention, but I am thinking of that terror of the evil eye that had the inquisition insisting on accused witches entering their presence backward.

"My familiars call me Silesia." I give my name.

Feigning exasperation she leans forward and speaks in a low voice to the nearest of the black guard.

Twenty seconds later a short balding man with olive skin approaches me, shakes my hand, backs away. Another approaches, this one gives me half a smile.

During the entire time they are introducing themselves, the light hangs in at head level. A benevolent watchdog, it broods as the last turns leading the fellowship from the room.

"Well! we meet, how nice." She makes it sound like sitting down to tea; we both take lemon.

So this is Silesia, I am thinking. Wise lady, good witch.

"Good!" she snorts, parrying my thought with supple rebound. "I'll tell you about good!" She halts a brutal little gesture by subduing it with the other hand, dropping them both in her lap. Her face takes on a satyric cast. "Under what conditions do you enter further into a room? Only lapsed Catholics hover . . ."

She is arrogant, obstreperous, immodest . . . "The kirkos, the hawk bears the falcon, the sun," she answers, patting the bed beside her in provocative invitation. Throwing her head back she laughs when I pull up a chair.

"Ahh! the air of restraint, I have encountered it before. The narrow relinquishment of the religious," she glances disparagingly at my lab coat, "no matter what the clothes."

At the frontiers of internal interrogation she is a tonic. And yet. I feel I should make some defense. She waves away my beginning comment with a gesture that says it isn't worthy, "A stoic is the only one who speaks ungracefully."

Perched high on the bed, shoulders overlapping the braced pillows, she seems bigger than life; I glance toward the foot of the bed for the bulge of her feet.

"Five feet ten," she says.

"I received your referral in clinic."

"They are like children."

"I didn't expect to be meeting here."

"One makes concessions."

Like a chess game, parry, parry, parry . . . "Do you mind my asking what's wrong?"

"You're free to read the chart," she shrugs, her eyes defiant. She seems to reconsider then and her tone softens, becoming slightly confidential. "I lacked patience and good old smarts, forgot to protect my back; a violence sent was returned, but I'll be fine."

She can be persuasive. I am estimating her age from the facial wrinkles and age spots on her hands at fifty. "Sixty!" she corrects, laughing violently.

In direct response to the laugh the other channel in my pelvis opens and the methodical turning of the fiery one begins. Startled, a small sound escapes me.

"Something happen?" her look is one of intense curiosity and when I do not answer she says, "A fate lends power to life."

When you meet the stranger who is no stranger it is always an event. What an intense individual! I am reminded of a painting by Remedios Varo, an oil on masonite of a small woman with dark hair, playing a sunbeam in a deep wood. She cannot help but influence the environment, she is so attuned to it; wearing the gossamer earth as cloak, concentrated fully, she draws her bow across the one beam of light piercing the forest. As she does, birds wake and leave their nests in the trees.

This woman sitting regally before me also relates the levels. Surely she is involved in magic, there is that knowledge in her of how to move the energy to and fro. And yet, sometimes it boomerangs. The thought fills me with perverse glee.

"Don't mock what you do not know!"

She also has some ability to read thought, "Well!" I say in my chipper-nurse style, "I think it's time to get back to work."

"Interview me," she throws it down like a gauntlet.

"You?"

"Why not? It's boring being cooped up here." Dropping the mythical for a moment she wrinkles up her nose and looks about in irritation and I find myself thinking, why not? . . . yes, why not, where a moment before I was ready to leave.

Vasti waves from the yard where Michael, bundled up like an eskimo, prattles to the dog, the kittens, a brave hen and the trees, "Have time to see the quilt I'm workin?" I leave my full water jugs at the fork in the path. "You been busy, havin ya?" her voice is soft, the glance she throws me, shy. I nod.

She removes Michael's bulk in the living room and he shakes himself as if testing that he is indeed free, then drops contentedly to play.

I follow her into a room full of bed. A south-facing window is covered in winter plastic. I watch as she lifts a long burlap bundle, placing it carefully on the coverlet. Walking to each of the four corners she unwinds.

"Ohh!" Something resembling a groan escapes me. Before me lies a geometric maze, a Chatres window in greys and blues. "Som isn sewn," she is tentative, unsure, "wha do you think?"

"Vasti, it's absolutely beautiful!"

"You like it?"

I am grinning like a fool. Her eyes light up. "It is good, isn it? It *is* good!" This time the words are firm and round.

As I am about to leave she mentions her Dad. "He nod been well ad all."

I trudge down hollow feeling guilty. I've been hurrying by in the evening hoping the old folks will not see me. It's been weeks since I stopped.

Tempi, answering my knock, does not say a word but grips my hand and looks with set face to the tiny dark form in the chair by the stove.

"I be fine," he says. But it is not so, and knowing it I tell them I'll be right back and hurry to the cabin for my tool bag. The blood pressure pounds in at a 258 systolic . . . the diastolic hitting in at 200.

"Dan, have you ever taken blood pressure medicine?" He gives me a wan grin that pulls his face down like a donkey's.

"He nod take em, they righ thar." Tempi points accusingly to a vial on a low shelf. "He take em if you say. You do Dad, righ? you take em if she say?" He nods wearily, not looking at either one of us.

While I check the prescription date and dosage a trace of the old grin returns, and an hour later when I get up to leave he grabs my hand and his eyes smile when I tell him I'll stop by tomorrow.

The mute worktable, the sawhorse, a small leaning sapling from which three branches have been struck . . . all sunk into the five inches of new snow, the white suspension that can be disastrous for the elderly.

That evening I am supposed to be writing a paper on Alliances and Processes in Family, but I don't feel well.

I decide to drive over the mountain to see Calamus.

She is alone. Seuell, who stays with her when she's in the area, has returned north. Iah is home with her husband. Morelle is in the apartment over the hardware with her visiting scholar. "Tell me about Silesia," I say.

"Don't you have anything you should be doing!" It is unlike her to be querulous, neither of us has a phone so there was no way I could have called ahead. I mutter something about being sorry and turn to leave. She pushes me down into a chair. "Forgive me! Where did you meet her?"

"She's a patient, in fact she's a patient of mine right now at the hospital."

She looks perplexed, then thoughtful. With an air of distraction she picks up the cat. "What happens to us shows us what we are." Methodically she starts doing skin rolls, doubling the soft fur back upon itself. The cat closes it eyes, lays down its ears and goes into a trance.

"We lived together, you know." The effervescent grey of her eyes grows dark, wary-like, radii from the center to the edges of the pupils. She searches my upturned face for a few moments then drops into the stuffed chair opposite, still holding the cat.

"We both taught in a secondary school in Shaker Heights, outside Cleveland. The *Provost Teacher* ran two ads, one for a sixth grade teacher here in Relief, and a part-time position for an adult evening class English teacher over in Serendipity. I was due for a change. Siles was nearing early retirement."

She shrugs. The cat makes a grumpy low sound at the suddenly vehement fingers digging into her pelt;

rising, she stretches, arching her back. Calamus laughs. "People change," she says, pulling the cat down, stroking her calm again.

She looks at me, "Do you know that Homer said Pallas Athene had the face of an owl? The same owl we associate with the western sky, the moon, the divinity of the dead?" I wait for a moment. It seems like a rhetorical question.

"What about pride, Cal?" The question bursts from me surprising us both. But, as I look at it lying there between us I realize that as much as I'm interested in the mythology of birds I am more fired with this intangible inner brew of questions.

"Pride?"

"Pride. Well, maybe it's not pride . . . maybe it's responsibility."

"You're not sure?"

I shake my head in confusion. "You talk about responsibility when you talk about honoring the Goddess. You speak about the individualness of the call, the need to keep the heart line clear. But, how, how do you know?" My voice has climbed a high mountain. "How do you know your inner convictions aren't prideful imaginings?"

"Suffering Lady! what's this prideful imagining stuff?" She looks at me teasingly. Then, her face grows serious, her tone gentle. "We don't, at first. We're not sure at all. It comes with time." She grows pensive. "You know, I wasn't brought up Catholic. I wasn't brought up to be anything at all." Her raised eyebrows are apologetic, "maybe I knew I was on my own from the very first.

"Bear with me though," she continues, haultingly,

"I've never looked at it quite this way until this very moment. Wouldn't too much fear of pride be antithetical to the assumption of responsibility for yourself? And, wouldn't the realization that you and you alone were responsible for your soul teach you damn fast to establish good communication? To hang back and call it pride, well, it seems to me, forces you to always hang back, because, of course," she looks sly, "it isn't entirely your responsibility. To take that would be prideful!"

"Direct contact?"

"Direct contact."

I am silent with the realization that I have always believed this.

"Wonder if they made her an owl because she was a creator deity? She gave birth, as a result no one could look on her face . . . in later times as the veil was dropped I can see she may have acquired the countenance of a night bird."

She is pensive. "All birds," she continues, "are symbols of rebirth because they are born twice. In Latin, the word for owl is strix, its inherited meaning, wisdom or Goddess."

The heat from the stove, the marginal singularity of her voice coming as from some far away country obscurely felt . . . the ease I suddenly feel . . . I blink heavily. I cannot keep my eyes open.

"Teressa! you look exhausted," she giggles.

"Must be the heat," I mumble, thinking vaguely that I have been exhausted ever since the exam on Silesia that afternoon.

Calamus is looking at me queerly, "I'll make coffee, but after that, I think we need a ritual. Yes, quite definitely, a ritual is in order."

"There are no barriers to mind, human will erects them . . . it is well to know when they should be employed."

"I always thought of energy as neutral."

"Oh it is." We have been sitting for an hour talking of many things. "As magic, it is nonpartisan, that's why it's so important that the person using it be grounded. I never meditated before becoming interested in the magical arts, but those first experiences!" she laughs, "well, they taught me—thank the Goddess they were funny—that I better get my act together.

"White and black sides of the spectrum . . . try to stay on the white unless you know very clearly what you're doing!

"There is a great diversity among us . . . white, black, every shade of grey. Some are terribly drawn to the black." There is wistfullness in her voice, her shoulders slump but straighten almost immediately. "Define Witch, someone's sure to jump in with an objection. I happen to think this is a healthy thing; if you begin to hear pronouncements from on high you've drifted from wicca. Ever seen the bumper sticker, My Karma Ran Over My Dogma?"

She takes a deep breath. "Remember, responsibility for yourself is all important. And remember, The Lady is always changing. Kirke makes no bones about where she stands . . . she's attracted quite a following. Not surprisingly." There is uncertainty in Cal's voice, "she's always been extremely canny about protecting her ass, maybe somebody was too much for her.

"From your appearance, I'd say we need to tie her hands, at least in relation to you. We might construct a fith. A fith-fath?" she looks up at my question and my sudden pacing, "it's a sort of resemblance of the person you want to keep in line, it doesn't harm them, it merely puts a constraint on them."

"Calamus, I knew her! It was a shock. Where I come from, it is said that to wake a new self is to wake a new responsibility."

"Wise saying."

The room over the living room is low ceiling'd and warm, there are pillows on the carpeted floor and a long, low bench holding three candles. "If you feel uncomfortable going skyclad wear this robe, definitely get out of these," she tugs the heavy sweater above my jeans. "Unconstricted is the word!"

As a concession to me she leaves while I undress, returning minutes later in an almost identical flowing gown. "First I want to make you a talisman."

The nubby cloth feels fresh against my buttocks as I sit on the woven mat and take the inch and a half diameter of thin stone in the palm of my hand. A tiny hole at the circumference pulls my finger. It is large enough to admit a fine cord, as I tilt the rock flakes of mica glitter in the light thrown by the candles.

"Some people prefer high altars but I always think of the Mother's altar as low and accessible, and like the underworld, full of visions. I'm going to paint the vortex tetrahedron."

On one side of the flat stone Calamus paints two triangles joined at the tip. One of the triangles she shades with black ink, the other she leaves the natural grey of the rock.

As we wait for it to dry we talk of magic. The "magic" that most know, power over an other, stage set for illusion, charlatanry. And then, the real stuff. Relationships cultivated with forms of being.

Turning the slim pendant over she writes REDIGO in red ink. "That will drive hunger and greed back whence it comes; you must protect your energy, you know. People who want your psychic energy do not send out warnings." She fastens the cord about my neck, "they wouldn't vampirise very many if they did! Become more aware of this," she carves an invisible circle before my belly and chest.

Reaching for a squat jar, she pours five wrinkled brown berries in my hand. "Eat one, the rest go back with you to the cabin where you will place one at each wall of the house. On the ground outside, when you place them, you will say, 'Of the rowan, power be to drive back!'"

"Remember, the power springs from within you but you must always be stronger than the power you evoke. Now, center down, I am going to draw the circle around us to contain what we raise. Pull it up with me from the Earth, but don't hold to it, always let it flow . . . always let it flow. When the Mother replenishes, there is no end to it . . . when we are through, go home and go to sleep."

CHAPTER 16

I don't sleep. Grateful beyond words for Calamus' grounded tuition I return to "owl" but do not sleep. The coursing molecular serpent has risen opposite its sister, the light-filled golden one; I am a field of irregular spasm, painful retraction of nerve and muscle, and gastric distress.

These notes may piece together a kind of picture if I remain calm. For the affliction to be so pervasive it must be deep. Probably at the neuronal synapsis level of the central nervous system. That network of cell bodies, axons, dendrites and junctions that carry information throughout the body.

In this world of basic transmitting blocks the impulse can be stopped, made to echo, stutter, chant rhythmically or arrhythmically. I have the sense of being in the throes of cellular alliteration.

The tiny bodies of the neurons, the number of dendrites, these are being changed. The size of their axons, the number of pre-synaptic knobs and terminals, the dual flow of liquid gold and fire is re-arranging them.

The transmitter substances that cause action potential, depolarization, increase in membrane permeability, this microscopic world weathers the dance by altering.

Sodium ions, whirling confused, do not flow freely and since they do not diffuse as they have for eons, essential electronegativity within the neurons does not decrease.

A terrible panic searches my flesh. Three thousand molecules of acetylcholine in each transmitter vehicle . . . enough vesicles in each terminal to transmit ten thousand impulses . . . I try to quiet my frightened child with clinical detachment.

Since I cannot pray through the simultaneous firing of so many synapses, whether there be a summation, spatial or otherwise, and whether it occur over the entire membrane concurrently, is not up to me.

It is nine a.m., both channels have closed. The two different yet one energies are back in their pelvic cave, my state of alarm subsides. I need to eat something but cannot take down more than half a brown banana without nausea.

I've been wrung out and left to dry in a freezing gale. My skin looks like a plucked chicken. Piloerection it is called; oh, if I had fur wouldn't it be a bounteous mane! hair follicles on end, engaged in waving and trapping the warm air.

As it is I'm extremely bumpy, pale and cold as a corpse. The cotton of my bra is suddenly sandpaper against tender breasts and sore nipples. No way can I function in the hospital today!

Vasti's party line is busy. She says she will "keep on it" until she gets through and leave the message with Mrs. Kane. She is the soul of tact, never inquisitive, but her look is worried as she tells me to go back to bed.

I need air and walk down the hollow with my face gratefully up to the thin sun. Dan is still sitting in the chair by the warmest wall, but the twinkle in his eyes is back. He tells me I look worse than he could ever look.

"Thanks," I respond dryly, watching him take another dose of his medicine. Hurl is taking him to town to see the old doc this afternoon. He will be OK. It is not yet his spring to die.

Walking slowly along the watercourse under the slate overhang I come upon a hedge of bog myrtle and sit down right in the middle of it. It is only now scattering oblong dried leaves as if new green tips were needed to push the old growth off. Keeping to the shade it has thrived. In the wet the birds have not bothered the flea repellant, insecticide berries; half a dozen clusters hang untouched.

Sitting there gazing at the untouched berries a few inches from my nose I remember Calamus' rowan, those dried little pods she advised I place around the house.

Well . . . it would certainly seem that my house under fire from within should at least be protected from without. Digging into my pocket I find the berries in the dusty far corner. Pulling up, I continue the climb. When I reach the cabin I place two on the north and west sides directly in snow, and two on the south and east between the exposed cropped grasses.

Our head nurse turns to me after finishing report, "Do you know your isolation technique?"

I'm hesitant, "It's been a few years."

"That's something you don't forget."

I grunt acknowledgement. I'm very tired. I bought rice bars on the way into town thinking they if anything would go down easy. I've been popping an inch or two of calories into my mouth every half hour in lieu of the usual lunches. This does not seem to disrupt my stomach.

"As I told you during report, it's a blood disease, very rare. Not being an airborne menace, no mask is necessary. Doctor feels it better she not know, if she asks, we're awaiting the total profile." She speaks with rapid jerky movements of her hands that leave the impression she would be only too happy to float away to a crisis somewhere else in the hospital.

Standing outside Kirkan Neere's door, with its red isolation warning sticker, suited up like a soft shell astronaut, I take a deep breath and push ahead.

There are no visitors. The striped amber eyes, forever flickering, rest on me with curious solvency as from the belly of the whale. "Well! I've missed you," she smiles. The eyes flash. Suddenly, something specializing in calm, waves a hand over the crescendo. The sparks grow limpid, almost forlorn. "Do you see what they've done?"

I look at her steadily, "How are your three bodies?"

"O Goddess, thank you!" Chortling, she throws out her arms, "they've been sabotaging my virtue, I need the elements, they're not found here! They believe their bilious pleasure is to war with all pomposity against the consciousness of immanence.

"It's the lack of barriers, isn't it?" she leans forward, "poison and peril to them the lack of barriers in the innately active, constantly changing, metamorphosing Being that is life."

I catch myself grinning, "I think I smell sulphur."

"You find me tendentiously wayward?"

Chewing my collected thought, while I unwind the stethoscope within its isolation sleeve, I postpone answer. I am thinking of how free thought can be when it is still a clandestine activity.

"Begin where you are, not where you think you should be!"

The earpiece of the stethoscope on their way to my ear, I stop, surprised. The message is claraudient.

"See!" she laughs at my surprise, "the third eye

opens, but there are other tangible ways of knowing. The lack of mind barrier that so confounds . . . it is nothing to the twin consciousness." She looks at me, weighing something. "Some sense of timidity holds you back." And then, in answer to my thought, "I nip and tuck around the vortex but that doesn't make me evil."

"It means nothing to me."

"Oh, I think it does." She raises herself up in the bed. "These hospital beds are impossible . . . they're launching a whole barrage of new tests . . . "

The verbal, as lavish as it is paradoxical, eddies while I work. Holding admiration for her verbal pyrotechnics uppermost in mind, I attempt to channel my fundamental attention in another direction entirely. I think of a comment Jean Cocteau made in *Diary of an Unknown* . . . about a painter inverting the work in progress in a mirror, to highlight the mistakes she's made.

The slim, stone medallion flops back and forth on my sternum as I make the bed. "You are learning quickly." I am so preoccupied with shuttling back and forth between Cocteau's real and mirror image, that I have forgotten her presence. "All I grasp is a name," she says, "Cocteau . . . the rest is a blur."

"It is intriguing," I am reluctant to admit the high I experience knowing this can be done.

"Enthusiasm never hurt," her expression is dour. "Did you know that the real meaning of the word discipline is to take something in, until, comprehending it fully, it becomes part of your living consciousness?"

There is noise outside in the hall, she glances at the

door and then back at me. "Miss Teressa Mark, tell me the truth. What do they say is wrong with me?" Her gaze is unwavering.

If the bear in the cage asked me to open the door and I could do so without being mauled . . . well, there really is no question.

"They say you have some rare blood disease."

"How long do they think they'll hold me?"

"Two weeks at least."

"Well." She takes this in calmly. "We'll have to change that. You must come and visit me, I have rare assemblages of herbs. Out my way spring comes early."

The door to the room is thrust open and an aide shouts my name. When I step out, she hisses, "they called a code on Mr. Craig." Pointing like Custer directing a charge she says, "211, pronto!"

A controlled frenzy funnels staff and equipment into the door at the far end of the hall. Slipping off gown and gloves, I follow. I catch sight of Mr. Craig's face as they heave him in the air to allow placement of the board. It is as calm as a baby's. You made it old man, I think, you made it just fine!

Twenty-five cc's of sodium bicarbonate is thrust at me along with a large syringe and an intracardiac needle, "draw it up!" "Make way! make way!" The defib machine roars into the room.

As I back up against the wall the cool liquid vial in one hand, the syringe in the other, the old man's smile is like a concrete presence in my breast amid the pandemonium.

I view the screen with its level line quietly for a minute, then, walking over to the neighboring over-bed table, I place the articles I'm holding down. Turning, I walk out of the room.

An hour later . . . "They said you had an attitude problem in Pediatrics," my Head Nurse's eyes are accusing, "it was in your report."

"He begged not to be subjected to that."

"You think he knew?! you think he knew at that point! What difference does it make, didn't make any difference to him! Staff needs the experience . . . and while you're staff of mine," her face is belligerent, "I expect you to follow orders!"

We are released early. The paper on Humoral Factors vs. Nervous Factors in the Control of Respiration During Exercise, has chance of being completed before dinner. That will leave the hour after for studying The Dermatome Segmental Fields of Sensation. As I drive I plan, before I tie into Suspension Stability of Chlomicrons in Lymph . . .

Easing into heavy traffic on Main Street, the floor of the little car vibrates. As I follow a blackened coal carrier, metal grinds. The suspension leaps and rattles. Inches from a gargantuan rear mudflap, a wide black bumper closing up the rear view window, I sit sealed within the noise and fumes. I drive my toy car among the blackguards.

Hemmed in as I am, engine idling, waiting for the truck ahead to move, I thumb through my book bag. Sudden light on my blind fingering tells me traffic has started up. Pushing in the clutch, throwing the gear lever into position, I lurch after the truck now putting distance between us.

Vibration increases. Under my feet there is a wordless shudder as my center of gravity tilts. I feel the scouring of the blacktop in my bones.

Whooosh of truck brakes behind me, on top of me. Truck doors slamming. I am suddenly surrounded by laughing smiling faces.

A man opens my door and helps me up. An authoritive base voice says, "it's a tie! Suras sundown" "What is it a '79?" "Thay go like tha ya know." "Lookit tha road" Three men lie down under the front end, "Ahh! ya shood see it, rus righ through!"

"Hey Bob, wha ya folks all doin, havin a party?" the sheriff has appeared at the edge of the circle of interested faces, all traffic has stopped. "Well, we all stop ya know. Have ta. This lady here, she have a mite of a problem."

"Well, you gotta do sompin about it," the sheriff says, his jowls working, "ya gotta move it, miss, it's holdin up everythin, and the busiest time of the day too!"

"I'll have to get a tow. . . "

"This wee thin?" a young burly guy on my right is grinning. He elbows his friend, "Mother! nutting here a few gud men can't handle!" There is bawdy laughter.

Someone takes my arm and eases me back. The Pinto's door is shut. Half a dozen men circle and, bending, grab her below her faded blue apron. She rises Sultana-like. After traffic is pushed even farther back to allow passage, she is carried from the road to a short blind alley half a block away from the hardware and settled with a thump in the dirt.

I thank, and I thank some more. Finally, reconnoitering some things from the car, I close her up sadly wondering what it will cost to fix her. When I turn blinking from the alley to the normalized street, Morelle is standing on the pavement grinning at me, her hand in a young man's pocket.

"Well! we saw all the excitement, little did we know it was you, Teressa!" I groan, belaboring the problem but she cuts me off, "pooh! it can be fixed, I want you to meet Zachary Segal." Humorous eyes with light brown tints in them look at me from behind no-rim glasses. A long hand grips mine.

"You're coming home to dinner," Morelle continues— Zachary's grip agreeing—"and from there we'll arrange for a garage," she grins at the two of us. "It's all settled." One on either side, they hustle me along the sidewalk.

The door to their apartment, to the side of the main entrance to the hardware, opens on an M. C. Escher juggernaut, three avenues of climb confronting me. Morelle steers around my hesitation, "two lead nowhere, they never got around to taking them down."

I follow up ten steps, the stairs that run escalator-like over a rail to my left deadend at a wall, ours continue to climb, turn and meet a door, veering away from a third set which, abutting a corner, rise sharply through a plastered area in the ceiling.

She fumbles with keys. Air rushing out on the tiny square landing is drywood and dusty with a hint of resin. "It used to be storage area for the people below, could drive right up the embankment out back. Tore out miles of shelving," Zachary's voice at my elbow is proud. "Couldn't part with that wood, those were boards, *real* boards. You know what lumber costs today? Scrappy little pieces, all knot and warp!"

"Just look," he is waving his arm in a panoramic gesture and leading me to a dark wooden pulpit at the same time. "Climb up here and look.

"It was just an empty room," he calls from below while I stand with my hands on the curved symposium, surveying. "We drew the walls on the floors first with marker pen; it took a while before we could agree," his glance is roguish as he stares off in the direction of Morelle's noise, "but when we did, we sanded and stained and fixed them in place, three-quarters height, for unobstructed heat flow."

Morelle is snapping on lights, the silver hair coming into view as she goes from room to room illuminating the layout, making it come alive, until it looks like the mockup of a city, or a playhouse minus its roof.

Some of the cubicles have colorful Indian drapery and hangings suspended in tent folds over their headspace. I think of fairy tales and inscriptions on old books. In places where the wall dividers run almost to the ceiling a rim of light outlines the area like a narrow ermine muff. It is from one of these that Morelle's voice floats out, "What does she say?"

Zachary is waiting for my response. "I, I've never seen anything like it . . . it's special!"

"She says she likes it . . . it's special."

"Hummnn . . . I knew she'd like it." I hear her speaking, but cannot make out anything further. A few minutes later she surfaces from the maze bearing a tray and gesturing us through another series of walkways to a room. "Wine, cheese and crackers; it's all arranged, Nat's going to look at your car, he'll call later and let us know."

"They're like muscles, unflexed, they become quite useless . . . " Morelle plops a broccoli floret into her mouth.

Zach's absorption in her mouth is pointed, "I decided to include the Appalachian worker in my sabbatical research to insure this woman here doesn't become isolated from reality. She seems inordinately concerned with psychic muscles."

"Not inordinately," her answer, scrambled as it is through food, is warm; her eyes under raised brows, teasing.

A little after six I place my empty bowl on the plank table and sit back with the remnants of my wine, I must be up and doing something about that car, I tell them, and find a place to stay for the night, maybe a few nights. "Stay here!" their joint response is enthusiastic.

They outdo each other stressing how fine it would be. I falter. I stress the crazy hours . . . so much studying, I say. They become even more vociferous and are making such noise that we do not hear the apartment door open, nor footsteps enter and progress along the maze toward the dining area where we sit.

"I knocked but you're making a lot of noise!" The deep voice is amused. The speaker standing at the door has half his face in shadow; light falls on the crooked ironic grin and relaxed shoulders.

"Nat!" Morelle jumps across the room throwing her arms around him in affectionate familiarity, tugging his hands, drawing him into our circle. "You haven't eaten, there's plenty. I want you to meet Teressa."

He nods at Zach, the grin if anything growing more lopsided. Watching him submit to Morelle's nurturing I feel a curious hum. All parts of ego—the vital, astral, mental bodies, will occasionally cohere, the etheric double, emotions and thought, forming a composite. The reality, when you encounter it in another, hits the diaphragm a welcome punch. It doesn't happen often.

The face above me is in repose, the grin faded, and from some timeless place I find myself in Persia, first millennium b.c. I am under one of a hundred great bull columns of the larger palace at Persepolis. The Goddess pillar fuses symbolism with the kneeling bull, the animal's long majestic head, adorned with the spirals of the crescent moon; Ishtar's rosettes ride like a shield on his forehead.

"Humor her! scouring Main Street with the broken metal of the car didn't go well with her this evening." Morelle has a hand on my shoulder.

The genuine pleasure in his eyes makes me uncertain. For want of something to say I babble something about adding water. He simply bends and takes my hand.

Glancing from one to the other Morelle says, "You two know each other?"

"We haven't rightly been introduced." The teasing retort is for her, but the grey wolf eyes are all for me. Seeing the look she jumps into introductions. "Nathanial Auchin . . . Miss Teressa Mark, Teress, my cousin Nathanial; Nat owns Caruther's garage."

CHAPTER 17

Following an unreasoning wind, spirals tall as ghosts kick snow feet at the pickup and when we pass Dan and Tempi's porch, rounding the bend into blackness, more snow forms collide; a convocation in the lee of the land, they whirl on us for tunneling through their midst.

"The Bakers are good people," his eyes strain through the white. Under the basketball hoop he leans across me and slams the door with the flat of his hand, "sticks, pick you up at seven?"

By the time I reach the front door the truck's headlights are mounting jerkily toward the main road, I watch as they turn left, climb and disappear over the mountain.

Once he told me he was living temporarily at his brother's place just up the road and could ferry me easily back and forth, my choice was to return to "owl" where all my papers and books lay about in orderly disorder.

I am glad to be back. Why am I walking then disjointedly from room to room? "Owl" has never felt so lonely, I am unable to start any of the half dozen projects.

I fill the kettle. I pour an inch of brandy in a chunky little jar with blue flowers that once held cheese. The stove belches and I listen to it murmur as the fire steadies. Pulling the old rocker into the dark corner by the window I drop Beethoven's piano concerto in E flat in the cassette recorder.

The cadenza having been reworked, the orchestral march completed, the piano notes are The Shekinah. They have never been Emperor to me. This is The Beloved allocated to the inner worlds with all their pathos and estrangement. This is The Beloved sent apart from The Face.

The pianist plays the immeasurable sorrow, the

struggling to comprehend, with sensitivity, and eventually, with exuberantly joyful acceptance. Here is victory. Here is the truth of being caught in the polarity worlds while holding to the unreckonable Face.

I am looking at the dark shape of the pine outside the window when both channels open. Rising together, touching, repelling, in that spiral dance I am beginning to recognize, they rise to my navel; there, light and fire of a thousand suns, they spin the childbearing.

A picture flashes on the mind's retina of a red birthing room used six thousand years ago. This time, caught up in the dance, we whirl at a different level.

The pair does not progress together past my navel. There is hesitation that I know as intensity of heat and a blaze of light as opening consciousness flowers; but then, the burning liquid one recedes alone to the pit where it curls in upon itself and the other follows.

That night the disequilibrium is more than I can bear and I fall back upon the thought of former years and bring myself to explosive orgasm half a dozen times. The smoldering subsides somewhat, but in its stead I am possessed by a nameless urgency.

I make tea and toast. Taking two Darvon Compound capsules, my head full to bursting, I finish Humoral Factors and review chlomicrons, and then fall asleep and sleep the sleep of the dead for four hours.

At five, I leap out of bed before the alarm and sit in blessedly uneventful quiet for twenty minutes. As I wash up, breakfast and review some more of the day's work, I deliberately do not think of Nathanial Auchin.

"She woan hurt you, she's shy, jus nudge 'er over."
There is no need, the pig—it is indeed a pig—sitting up beside him at seven a.m., sees me climbing in, burrows her snout hurriedly under his arm and huddles as close to him as she can.

"Her name is Grindle." His eyes sweep over me approvingly, "you look nice." I smile, I mean what with the competition and all, I'm flattered. But I'm too busy holding my seat apart from the barrel of pinkish brown to comment. The old truck lurches forward. As we leave the ruts of the hollow and make the right hand turn onto the road, Grindle loses it; not having feet placed as mine solidly on the floor boards, she rolls to the right like a hard-boiled egg on a counter.

Keeping her eyes fastened on Nathanial Auchin, ignoring my presence, she grunts and leans on my thigh and knee. "She got herself in such a snit at me leaving this morning! foolish ol girl!" he fondles her ear, "thought as how I'd take er to the garage for the day. She can watch the ol geezers. Ya like that don't ya? pick up a few tidbits?" the pig listens to his voice.

She's baby-blanket pink dipped in milk chocolate, brown splotches on her sides. Queen-mother, right regal like, she sits now with her long snout in the air looking out over the dash at the road ahead. The cab smells of straw and mace and clover.

I sneak a look at Nathanial Auchin. He starts whistling, seems quite pleased with life. Carrying pigs to market is I think the expression. There are no stars visible this morning. His nose is too long, anyhow.

Bouncing over the rutted curve at the foot of the

mountain I think of Thalak and crane my neck, catching sight of a few wisps of wood smoke—the kind you see when someone's just fired up her stove of a morning. I'd like to see her. I could walk down on my day off.

Thought is interrupted by a moist suction against the skin of my cheek where it passes over the mandible. I do not budge. Grindle's snout is up against my face. She sniffs, and each time she inhales my skin waffles lazily. It's such a funny sensation, I laugh.

She does not bolt, she cocks her snout, the better to see you, my dear, and two wise little eyes meet mine. "She likes you," he glances from the road to the two of us again, "do me a favor? check out my brother? He's in room 211, tell him you saw Grindle and she's OK."

"I'll go up after class. I, I appreciate your taking me home last night, I got a lot of work done that I wouldn't have finished at Morelle's . . . as much as I wanted to stay . . . "

"I know what you mean, not your own place, I miss mine on the Wyliot. Bob's got livestock that need tending, he don't trust them to just anyone. Figured he'd get better faster if he knew they were being taken care of, but I'll be glad to get back home."

His eyebrows are going white from the bottom up and the stiff colorless hairs refuse to lie down. I find myself watching the corner of his mouth, so lopsided and vulnerable, where it runs into the clean shaven jaw.

At the hospital, arm across the pig and me, hand on the door, the grey eyes are only inches away. I think of a peculiar type of moss I've found on old hemlock that I like to rub my cheek against. The pupils do not waver, "six?"

"Well now, Miss, that's righ nice of you," the man in the bed looks me over, "you say she was sitting up there alongside of you? She nod gunna wanna stay ta home when I get back. Nat, he spoil er!"

"He didn't want you to worry." Dashing down the stairs I have just discovered Kirke's empty room. The isolation sign had been removed. I was flabbergasted when, poking my head in I found the room empty, cleaned and ready for patients. "I've got to get back, Mr. Auchin. I'm glad doctor says you're doing better."

His eyes are measuring, "he going to give you a lift again?"

"This evening I expect . . . "

"You watch yerself, Miss, he used to having his way with the ladies, my big brother Nat, snaps iz fingers all he does."

How does one respond when confronted with brotherly love? Leaving him, I poke my head in at the nurse's station, "what happened to Kirkan Neere?"

"Discharged. Her blood tests all came back normal. Kinda strange." She looks up from the charts, mouth pursed, her eyes skeptical. "It's odd that so many different chemistries could be so far off and yet suddenly revert to normal just like that!" She snaps her fingers.

"The lab? A mistake?"

"Not likely . . . not so many. Ahh! who knows. Anyway, she wouldn't let them take more blood for repeats. Dr. L. was pissed, but we had to let her go."

"Maybe, what's maybe?" the quiet questioning look does not hem 'n' haw. Neither does mine, the look I give him is steady but I soften my voice, "maybe is maybe." I have nudged Grindle over, shoved is the more accurate word, but she refuses to budge so I am squashed up against the metal of the door, annoyed he has not pulled his true love over. He doesn't put the truck in gear nor drive away from the hospital.

My Celt is rising, it takes effort to keep my voice soft, "I have a lot of work to do this weekend, it would be much better for me if we left the question of dinner hang until next week." I hadn't intended that petition slip in at the end. He hears it, nods, and we are moving; Grindle sighs and lays her contented head in my lap.

When we arrive at "owl" his slam on the recalcitrant door is a bit much; "Monday at seven?" I nod.

"Teress?" Climbing the path, the first time use of my name hits like a bolt. I turn. He and Grindle look up at me from the passenger side of the truck; a big puff of steam appearing next to a smaller puff-puff. "Weather coming, better keep the stove fired up."

I'm brim full of sadness and if someone asked me why I couldn't answer, nothing but a death in my immediate family could so fill me with gloom. Is this the way decisions arrive? Invading, cloaked as monumental archetypes? This has got to be more than disappointment, more then disillusionment; it is scary. I look ahead and I cannot see myself.

Opening the door after finishing my supper I pull the rocker near the hot stove and sit gazing out into the dark. It is utterly still and heavy, like an introduction to the work of D. H. Lawrence I read once, that killed the writer's opus. I am going mad, I think, thoughts crazy, kangaroo-pole-vaulting about.

Arise in the midst of the night and commune with thy God, the Koran says, and ego will be put down, knowledge will be given thee, and thy path smoothed. Replacing a full cold kettle atop the stove, I glance around at the order and warmth and climb to the loft.

Heat rises warm on the meditation cushion. This business of contemplation, this need of my flesh for the silence, this fits into Iah's "it's not what ye know it's what ye be!" This one thing has convinced me there is something in reincarnation. Because, I didn't learn this. The need has been within me for as long as I remember.

Attribute your power to that which you have as objective or shield. Breathing slow and deep, I sink into my "obsession" and wait. I don't wait long, out of the void, stillness moves into flesh, calming and erasing the personality of forty years. A glow approaches that is incredible truth and joy. This unutterable does not hold back, but flows over and around and through.

During one of the ecstatic "deaths" that evening, the light that has been coaxing the other from the cave, flows back into the pelvis like a child toward presents on Christmas morn. What new equilibrium is established?

Whirlwind of hidden and visible power, they rise together. I am somewhere apart from my brain, registering new information.

The mesencephalon and hypothalamus are especially active, pleasurable affective sensations bombard. The somatic cortex records the focal point of the barrage—nerve tissue in the pelvis. No pattern that is familiar positions the experience in memory.

The association areas in the thalamus and those around the cortex shift nervously in their struggle to process; like sellers on the floor of the New York stock exchange, moments before the crash. When it comes, the crash takes out the sellers, the electronic data machines and the Big Board. There is no market for the energy that follows.

It is two a.m. when I lower myself gingerly down the stairs to feed the stove. Every muscle in my body aches. Bones wobble as if buffeted by vacillating currents. Pulling on the light I sit dazed, close to the heat.

I don't know how long I sit. Soft scratching on the door attracts my attention. It takes all my strength to open the simple clasp, my fingers are so uncoordinated, and when I do two kittens fall all over each other in their hurry to get inside.

Shivering from cold I stare blankly out into the blackness. Something in the silence draws me. Pulling on my coat and hat I pick up the old wool blanket from the back of the rocker.

Nothing stirs. Under an opaque and starless sky I climb up behind the cabin, drawn to the rough slope and the stand of old hemlock. Jutting upward at an impossible angle, established on a tortuous series of ledges, they have never been cut.

I have to crawl. Up to the roots of one old mother I pull myself and when I reach her I wedge myself between her bumpy, exposed knees, covering my head and shoulders with the wool blanket; I am every child hugging the Earth, curled within her, pulling up healing. The pain subsides, peace falls like a fine white coverlet.

The sound of kittens lapping milk is comforting, as comforting as the dirt clawed on the hillside—forever altering. Exhausted and chilled I climb back into bed.

I dream, I dream that naked, I am crouched on hands and knees like a dog in a deep field of manure. I am struggling, unable to get my footing, my breasts dragging back and forth in the slop, the turgid muck sensuously smearing my belly.

Everything is hopelessly slippery. Wallowing, I hear laughter. A man is approaching to the rear of me. Coming up behind, taking purposeful wide steps, a man in barn boots walks toward the two white quarter moons of my butt. He is laughing, naked, very large and very erect.

I feel the wash of him. Hear the sucking as he pulls me free with two strong hands; lifting my rear out of the mire he gives a loud sigh of satisfaction. I wake at the crest of climax.

A dirge tolls unceremoniously and for the remainder of the night there is no sleeping. I seem to be permanently chilled and this thought dislodges some forgotten information on hypothalamic overstimulation. I am not interested, if you no longer know who you are, whether adrenergic exhaustion has set in or not, is no concern at all.

Pulling my attempts at keeping a journal into bed with me, I huddle. I read about a woman—no one special really, though she often thinks she is—who finds herself entering a monastery. Only to lose the self she finds? Is this the postscript?

No doubt, the tenor of the more recent notebooks has changed. When I am finished reading, I do not center down for fear of what will rise, I sit as calmly as I can, waiting the light.

Dressing when the skies pink, I drink molasses in skim milk, pack two sandwiches and extra sweaters in a small duffle and, leaving "owl," walk out to the road.

It is crisp walking, the movements of birds about in the early morning and my feet pressing and packing the snow is the only sound. Just before Dan's house I notice another, the sound of a great snake dragging herself down the slope above and to my left. I round the bend quietly, keeping my eyes on the slope.

Forty feet above, on a trajectory that will bring him out at his workhorse, Dan bends determinedly around a twenty-foot tulip poplar. I halt, shaking my head in disbelief. His arm goes up in greeting.

The sight of him restores me, I quicken my pace. When I emerge from the frozen swamp at Thalak's I have come to a decision.

"Are you OK?"

"Yes!"

She looks unbelieving and catching my shoulders, pulls me forward. "Come in, come in."

Thalak is shaking her head and the motion tugs the mass of her hair over the flannel across her shoulders. "Dear young thing," holding onto me she walks me to the mirror in the short hall leading to the kitchen. "Look at yourself, look, then tell me you're OK."

The woman in the waverly glass stares at me with eyes that near pop out of her head. She looks like she's cried battery acid, deep crevasses incise her cheeks. Her neck is gaunt, there is no luster in her hair and she has an angry red rash sitting like a mad butterfly over her nose and forehead.

I feel wooly just looking at her. That can't be me! That woman is mad, anyone can see that.

As Thalak moves past to the kitchen I look again. I steady on the ruined eyes, there is less shock this time. I muster a degree of clinical detachment. Behind the evident destruction something so vast stares back at me that I wince.

Instantly a wave of emotion catches me up in a sentimental wash. Tears well up behind the puffy red rims in the mirror. Perversely, I wrench myself from the fluid emotion. There is something curious about it. Pulling free from the sentimentality that threatens to engulf, I look again in the mirror.

I look. I look as a baby looks at her toes before she knows they're hers. I do not pull up courage to face this void, I pull emptiness. I look past the accidents of the woman I have come to recognize as myself. I let her drop.

Advancing past the eyes in the mirror, I meet the most unbelievable, incomprehensible smile.

I am laughing when Thalak appears again beside me. Her eyes catch the two in the mirror and they are mine again, "What is so funny?"

"Life. I look like I've got a thyroid condition, don't I?" I grin at her in the crooked glass. "And your nose looks like a ski jump. Thalak, I need to ask a big favor."

An hour later as we get into her car she turns to me, "Does this man we are going to see know anything?"

CHAPTER 18

We are three hundred miles from Relief. A short lay brother is looking at us shrewdly, "It is customary for those wishing an interview to write or phone for an appointment."

"I'm very sorry, I realize I should have... it's kind of an emergency..."

His eyes are weary, "the emergencies of the world soon pass on to other emergencies."

To my left Thalak's irritation surfaces in an orgy of foot stomping, clumps of snow from her boots rapidly piling up on the carpet at his feet.

The brother's unruffled face creases, "if you will please remove your boots, put those slippers on," he points to a box with a sign over it, "I'll call Father Bruno and inquire if he will see you," he glides off over the spotless floor.

"When you heard Camaldolese you probably thought stone shelters, wild outcrops, high peaks . . . or thatched cabins in deep woods, hummnn?"

He is right. Just as, hearing his footsteps approach, I figured a big man; he isn't much taller than me, he just puts his feet down like statements.

After warmly bustling Thalak into a room with a pot bellied stove and a soft armchair, he and I have continued along the corridor to the kitchen of the guest house. He is now rooting around in the adjoining pantry.

"I haven't eaten either," he yells, "your timing is perfect! Aahah! I've found it, I knew there was a loaf of french left. Brother Midas hides it," he emerges waving a long crusty loaf of bread over his bald pate. "Thomas Aquinas says that souls embodied cannot behave as if disembodied. A lot of our problems arise from the very fact that we do."

"So, young lady, it sounds like both channels have opened. Wonderful! we toast to this!" he lifts his glass.

Thalak shoots me a look that says, dotty, but pleasantly so, better than the brother at the door. Her face is flushed from the heat of the wine and the stove.

"A very solid basis in reality is needed at this stage. Remember," he waves a finger at me, "what the 'Dumb Ox' says, we can't move ahead through these adventures in consciousness without a healthy, grounded body.

"We've got to correct the lopsided association some of the most right-minded folks have developed of ethereal spirit-stuff. Vastly overdone, vastly overdone. Embodied is the word to remember." Thalak is watching him now with real amusement.

"Yin-yang," he continues, "not light-dark or male-female but heavenly-earthly," he pushes a raw carrot about his plate like a dugout, stabs it and chews. "Bound to be tension!"

"Remember," his jaws work rhythmically, "the two-way oppositional force that is at work, never lose sight of the contrariety. Perverse, utterly perverse to our limited way of seeing it. When the polarity grips you, grabs you like this," both broad hands are on his neck in a choke-hold, "and you can stare it in the face and see both sides, then you are liberating thought for all of us. Our view is foreshortened, otherwise we would see along the road to where they intertwine.

"You know," his light brown eyes are warm, "our fates do not always take our plans into consideration. They may be good, our plans, don't get me wrong, but if the work the world soul would have us do is not the one we personally choose . . . " he lets the sentence dangle and leans across the table. "You may have to fight yourself for your choice," the voice is firm. "Believe me, I know the conflict."

We are eating apple cobbler, "good isn't it? Bonaventure makes the best damn cobbler. "Well, the sexual . . . the alchemists had a better handle on it than we do in our day and age, they saw the need immediately for some degree of sublimation."

His gaze, so even and understanding, holds mine, "you've experienced the intensity, you think you're going to express that in any of the ordinary ways?" I feel myself blushing, "don't take it so to heart," he says, "don't take it to heart, we're all in this together." He waves my discomfort away.

"We're told we'll get heart problems, destruction of the spinal marrow, all sorts of sexual disorders, madness . . . said the same thing about playing with yourself when I was a boy." He shakes his head from side to side. "No one tells you about the true magic given to s/he who keeps the high point of contact open." The look he fastens on my face is full of gentle concern.

"Refuse to get sidetracked," he continues, "into personal magic or sorcery. The occult powers . . . we're all flattered by them . . . we're all children whose greatest talent, Anatole France says, is our ability to deceive ourselves."

"Did you know that alfalfa can put down fifty foot roots?" We've been driving in comfortable silence for an hour; Thalak gazing off into the late afternoon dusk that bodes changing weather, continues, "Amazing things roots! the methods of processing and handling differ from those one uses to retain the life essence in a seed."

"I've rented the old Barrick store. You know," she says in answer to my questioning look, "the little hole in the wall next the bank? Old man Barrick sold keys there, *when* he felt like opening. I figure," she does some mental arithmetic, "I'll have my fledgling business open well before tourist season. Not many make it into the interior but you wait and see, news travels and this root stock will be worth travelling for!

"Of course the mail order part will take a bit of work . . . and I'll need someone to help dig and replenish the stock . . . rotate the cured roots; be looking for a business associate," her profile has a childlike expectancy about it.

"Course, wouldn't want to pressure you, nothing in the world would make me do that! what with all you have on your mind, and, things I don't know anything about.

"Wouldn't be much in the way of earnings the first two years, just enough to keep the roof over your head, put food on the table, but after that I believe it will more than pay for itself. Have savings that will take care of overhead until it gets on its feet."

Having said her piece she hums a lilting threepenny tune, fingering the beat against the tartan of her coat. I reach across, take one of her hands in mine and hold it in silence. She doesn't look at me, "Maybe," her tone is light, "maybe you can think on it?"

"Yes," there is a catch in my throat, "yes, I will think on it! you knew I had decided, didn't you."

"Well . . . I don't read minds, I'm happy with more earthy energies, but I do notice you're not good at rationalization and I know from long experience that some realities will have no truck with certain others. Figured it was just a matter of time."

"I was about to ask if you would mind stopping at hospital hill." Tandy is the only one I feel I owe a verbal goodbye but she is not home and, standing before her silent apartment door, I realize there isn't much to say. I write a note wishing her good luck and telling her I am withdrawing from the program.

Leaving the motor running, I climb the back stairs to the hospital one last time. Withdrawing from the program effective immediately, I write the date and sign my name. There! one less body, one less future Certified Nurse Midwife for the dean to contend with!

This is it, I stand and look along the dark, deserted corridors with great relief, then, turning, run from the place that has no normal births. At the car Thalak looking at my face, laughs and begins talking about what she has in the freezer that would make good eating.

As I turn the car onto Swamp Road the glow behind the sea of dried cattails makes Thalak sit up and take notice, "Someone's at the house."

The windows are bright, and as we pull in the front door opens and a figure lopes forward. Cheshire-like white teeth in black face, Seuell leans over us, "And where have you two ladies been this late!"

"I was beginning to worry, she never stays out late any more, figured as how I'd get the place heated up and some soup thawed . . . " Seuell is pulling the afghan gently up to Thalak's chin, "said she was just going to rest her eyes didn't she?"

"I'm afraid I tired her out," I smooth the white hair back on the sleeping woman's forehead. "At least she had some of the soup, she kept telling me she wasn't tired."

Seuell harumphs, "Pretending, that's what she was

doing. And pretense don't go far at this age. So!" she turns to me, "you're not going to be a bone fide, certified midwife!" She has abandoned her frolicking, southern belle self and the look she fastens on me is wide-eyed and clear. "That calls for some of Thalak's brew!"

Disappearing down the hall to the kitchen she appears minutes later bearing a capped bottle before her like a scepter. Her eyes are dancing, "ya see I know where the stash is kept."

"As I rode out on a frosty night, silver wheel a-turning, turning, I met a Lady dressed in white, silver wheel a-turning, turning, . . . I had a suspicion she'd deliver on Candlemas; eight pound bouncing boy, vertex presentation, loved it! Had to leave the circle—a friend was being initiated—had to leave and drive up McMurdy Point. I vouched for her and then flew away on my broomstick to help Rita Meekin deliver her firstborn. It's a miracle each time," Seuell's face is full of wonderment, "and Rita so full of the Goddess from pushing that boy into the world, she lit up the room!"

We have been talking quietly by the table, accompanied by Thalak's soft snore from the couch. Seuell's forehead is cupped in the palm of her hand as she talks. "There was never any thought of me marrying him, that would have been a disaster! And, I certainly wasn't planning a family, not then, my applications were all in, I was going somewhere!

"Anyway, Mother insisted I continue with my plans, she would care for this eleven month old daughter I had suddenly brought into our midst, care for her until I finished school and got on my feet. She was ecstatic, really; my father's a pediatrician, she never had to work outside of the home."

Seuell's finger thoughtfully opens a square in the cold glass sweat, a little clear window into the red liquid, "It doesn't make me angry anymore, just sad. When you realize where blacks have been you understand their grabbing after whities's status, their hunger for his material goods. But shit!" her voice is decidedly angry despite her protest, "shit, I never expected a child of mine to choose that way!" her face is pained.

She fills my glass; fills her own, downs it in one gulp, fills it again. How many glasses of Thalak's homemade fire have I had? I have become convinced the black stove in the fireplace is breathing; I watch the belly go in and out, in and out.

Suddenly, I am crying, crying over hopes and plans down the drain.

I am vaguely aware of her chair pulling closer, feel the warmth of her round arm across my neck. "There, there! better now than later. I did that five years after graduation when I saw what it was going to take to wash the absurdity of the training away. Cried bitter tears, I tell you, when I found I'd sold myself for one cold mess o' porridge!

"Tess, you don't wanna climb that dung heap, there's nothing in the drug-surgery-interventionist medical model worth learning. You don't wanna be among the ranks, woman, insurance has gone too high, waaay too high!

"You cry it out now, you cry it out for all the oppressed who are lied to about being oppressed; people kept in ignorance and mystification, people alienated from their essential being." Her voice drops very low, "is you listening? Things are moving, you don't want to be part of the professionally elite system now."

She turns her palm over on the table under my nose, "spent years washing off what I picked up climbing that dunghill."

She hands me a tissue. The tears have washed away my last remaining shred of energy, I feel infinitely weary. "You know I was the first black woman to be accepted at my college. Made my folks so proud! Didn't wanna see, no one wanted to see." She sighs, "what an ostrich I had to become for the God of theory and practice, what a price I've paid!

"C'mon, I'm taking you home. You look beat and here I am going on and on . . . You ever want to do some births let me know, you'd be very welcome, I have more than I know what to do with, keeps me in food, and wood, and repairs on the car, and, . . . Rita being a tailor," she is grinning, "my next winter coat is assured." She's for real.

It takes a stilled mind to hear the song the world sings. The light is coming in the wrong window and there is humming in my head and all around me. I lie marvelling at how light I feel and the fact that I've slept 'til late afternoon.

Simone Weil once said something about St. Francis thinking he had been given an order to carry stones to Damian; she felt that as long as he was under this illusion, God wanted him to carry stones. Have I put my stones down? Did carrying stones fulfill something I wouldn't have dealt with otherwise?

Rolling over on my stomach I glance across the floor at the piles of work assignments: papers, exam guides, text books, assorted folders . . . each in the order of its scheduled appearance.

A wave of doubt engulfs me. I could collect those notes, have a go at catching up. At this thought nausea hits me hard and fierce, I lay back breathless waiting for it to subside. No, it is done; if a woman can't trust the body-wisdom at forty, what hope is there for her!?

I am happily puttering around my kitchen when footsteps sound on the porch and there is a tentative knock on the door.

Veronica's face is a sickly grey everywhere except the eyes, which are red-rimmed and puffy, "I have to talk to someone!" I am so surprised at seeing her that I stare dullard-like. We haven't been that close in class, I doubt we've ever really talked. She is flustered, her eyes liquid.

"She makes me so nervous, I couldn't remember the dosage fast enough, they've put me on probation," tears are streaming down her face. "Say I don't have the makings of a good midwife. Say, if I don't shape up I'm out?" there is disbelief in the voice. "I've tried so hard . . . I don't really know what else to do."

I can't think of anyone who will make a better midwife and I tell her this. "They've put Erin on probation too."

So this is the way it is going to be, harry a couple of the most sensitive, get them to trip, finally they will fall into a morass of self doubt; leave them there. How long has the school been doing this?

A chill goes through me. And these two women will

take it. Wanting to be midwives as much as they do, they will take the psychological battering, they will take everything that is dished out. Good Mother help us! And will they be able to heal themselves?

"Ronnie, are you sure you really want this?" She doesn't have to answer, the look says everything. That's it then, one more who must carry stones to Damian.

I haven't heart to tell her I've withdrawn, knowing instinctively that once I do the wall will be thrown up, I will no longer be the boon companion in similar shoes. I can't help thinking though that maybe they will leave off persecuting her when they find I've dropped out.

I watch from the window as she drives away, then, pulling on my hiking boots climb the ridge and walk and walk and walk until the day is but a wrinkle of light in the West. I have to find my way home in the dark.

CHAPTER 19

A vibrant plate within the interval is untuned, it plucks the frequencies from the birdsong; I turn over in bed irritated by the stridency of the monotonous sound.

I sit bolt upright! Nathanial Auchin, I forgot about him! It is seven a.m., Monday morning. The repeat action—at subdued intervals—of a truck horn drifts up the slope from the flat area by the basketball hoop.

Grabbing up my robe, I pound downstairs, jam my feet into the open boots by the door, scooping the laces inside the necks for safekeeping, and clump off to the green pickup.

He tries not to laugh. As I lumber up to the driver's window, the clear grey eyes, narrowing and crinkling at the edges, wrench wide in feigned innocence. He holds the look of a guilty owl for moments, then loses it. "Sorry!" he rasps . . . "sorry."

Gathering my convent-issue, coal-streaked terry about me with as much decorum as I can muster, I pull erect and wait. In an unfocused portion of truck glass I catch sight of the subject of the amusement, a tangled Medussa! the blush I've kept controlled at neck level rises.

He shrugs apologetically. Something resembling a whimper escapes his chest. He looks chagrined, at least, he tries.

"I'm leaving," I blurt out to punish him, "dropping out of the program . . . I've been sleeping a whole lot. I, I forgot you were coming," I finish lamely.

Wordless, wounded, haunted, isolated male . . . the change in him is immediate and thorough. The stare moves down to his hands, "you'll be needing your car, better get to work on that tie."

Hunched as he is behind the wheel he suddenly looks his fifty years, every one of them, and I am loath to have him leave. "Where's Grindle?"

"Bob's been discharged," he takes a deep breath and looks over my head at the sky, "expect freezing rain later in the day."

"Oh," my hand goes to the car's window ledge, "I hadn't heard about the rain . . . " I feel flustered and curiously abandoned there on the dirt . . . "I guess it wouldn't be a good evening for dinner then," I drop my uncombed head.

Staring at the high tire before me, I see the outer four inches are bald. "You have a wheel out of alignment," I say, as clumsy fingers right my chin and he leans out planting a kiss on the top of my nose, a kiss that smells of bay and allspice.

"Right!" the voice is gruff, "That's not the only thing out of alignment." He leans forward again and this time the kiss grazes my lips. Caution and vulnerability can go a distance but never compete with amazement; I am amazed at what I see in his eyes.

When did the snow melt? I stand on the cropped grasses by the porch relishing the simplicity of ground, twigs, pine needles, jagged bent weed; the beautiful understatement of her winter cover. Tawny golden umbers have it all over the more flagrant colors of summer. What will I wear?!

"There are only two diseases," Calamus is saying as she rubs my head, "one is riding an ass to search for an ass, the other is riding an ass and being unwilling to dismount. Compliments of ancient Chinese Master," she bows respectfully, and continues rubbing the elderflower and clarysage oil into my scalp.

Calling to Seuell in the other room, "you have the Johnswort?" she shakes my greasy head between her hands, "I'm glad, very glad you choose as you did! took courage."

"I met Hurl at the well this morning, he called it giving up."

"Well, we know better now, don't we?"

"He's not going to be the only one to say it."

Her eyes are tranquil, she shrugs, "half the work is in the resolution of conflicts, separating right from wrong action."

"Woman, you is goin to have murderous glints in your hair tonight!" Seuell bounces into the bathroom with a pint of clear red Johnswort oil. "Cal? run a hot tub? fill the sock full of the blackberry I cut in the gorge, nothing better for dull, tired skin!"

I groan, little trickles of oil seep through the flannel stocking she's tied about my forehead, "no offense, but you sure could use a pickup, woman! a light wash, then a primrose rinse to bring out the highlights . . . then, we go shopping."

"Going shopping" means we raid the attic. Between what we find there and Calamus' closet I am outfitted; I've never looked quite as colorful. They start with a heavy dark yellow linen skirt, long and brilliant as a Buddhist robe dyed in Bengal tumeric, with lighter tansy flowers embroidered about the hem.

"I don't know as I can wear this," I glance uneasily at the blouse they've given me, at the smooth mounds my breasts make under the fine, clingy silk; red as opium poppies, the blouse feels incredible. I feel incredible.

Calamus nudges Seuell, "you're going to wear it! that blouse and that skirt go together." "And this," Seuell shakes it out, "this is my best cape." She drapes a heavy wool burnoose in dark closed gentian over my shoulders.

"We forgot her feet!" While they scurry off I look at the woman in the mirror, oh yes, there are different realities, the woman in this floor length mirror is not the woman in the other.

Seuell returns with shoes and Calamus with boots, they measure the soles and decide. I am guided to a chair; the boots are pulled on, they fall in soft folds of leather, dropping to a mid-calf position when I stand, tucking up under the row of tansy buttons.

"Eureka!" Calamus crows. They step back with similar satisfied expressions as she digs deep in her skirt pocket. "These are special," she says, and clips tiny silver Isis wings on my ears.

"Knew you'd look like that if you ever got out of that social service drag!" the admiration in his voice is sharp and biting.

I want to say he looks fine in the charcoal grey suit but am overcome with shyness. I can only manage something brusque about the Citation being an improvement on the pickup.

"Couldn't take a woman to dinner sitting in Grindle's seat," the set of his jaw is amused.

The restaurant is overwhelming after the poverty of the cabin. Set high on a mountain above Serendipity, it is all dark wood and glass, an opulence of plant greenery and candle-lit tables overlooking the glitter of the town below.

There is nothing wordless, wounded or haunted about the man who talks familiarly with the maitre'd and guides me to a window table.

That night, the restaurant fills and the restaurant

empties and I am aware of it only as a backdrop of sound waves. When it refills with late nighters he orders more wine.

There is nothing special about his face. Watching him above the flickering candle I figure it's French Canadian surfacing by the arch of the nose, but the jaw, the jaw is too strong, the jaw is Native American.

A great ease has been floating between us as we talked. I recall a saying from an ancient text admonishing that no man be allowed at the making of a pot. I am surprised at my thoughts. This man could be allowed at the making.

"Events happen," he is saying, "Korea got me the Masters in Animal Husbandry but I never went after the veterinary license," he is toying with my palm, running a forefinger along my lifeline.

"Tickles"

"Hummnn. I've been working around cars for thirty years. When Grandpa Caruthers died and left me the garage I dropped the idea of the breeding farm . . . sometimes I wonder if I should re-activate that plan, I tell you, with these new cars a guy needs a degree in engineering, they want you to dump them, they don't want you to repair them."

I withdraw my hand and shift in my chair. It seems hot in the room. I feel his eyes roam over the poppy colored silk and ask myself what I want of this man. Do I know?

"How come you never married?"

I hear my answer and note the brusqueness. "Never met the right man; yours didn't last." I regret the comment immediately and place my hands in confusion on the table, "I'm sorry! that was uncalled for.

"Nurses don't have many illusions about marriage,"

I continue more softly, "too many confidences. Relationships between men and women are problematic, I don't know if they've ever been any better, maybe we just ask more of them.

"But you wake up one morning and the person you married is no longer there, you married a projection. Once you own the projection, the other becomes what he or she always was, certainly nothing you knew or wanted . . . "

"You've done a lot of thinking about this haven't you."

I don't answer for awhile. "Anyway, I'm different from other women, Nat. I have a vocation, a work to do," I search behind the wall of grey for the soul of the man, suddenly aware of how important it is to me that he understand.

"That you are!"

"Different things make me tick, I'm, I'm not much interested in the things that other women are interested in. You see, the part of me that is immortal is so very real," I hesitate, my eyes begging him to understand, "how shall I say it . . . it puts a well, different perspective on life."

He looks at me for a long time in silence, then, putting the candle to one side he rises, leans across and kisses me on the mouth. It is not a glancing kiss, it is slow and long and very thorough.

His eyes are very close, "Come home with me? They're about to throw us out, hear them?" he gestures over his shoulder, comically. Behind the double doors, kitchen cans are being pounded against each other as if someone is emptying the last of the garbage. Glancing around I see we are the only ones left, the large room has been darkened.

Vibrating bodies move in many different modes simultaneously. That's a phrase from the Order's manual on the use of handbells in the liturgy. We are sitting side by side in his den, boots off, feet up before us on pillows.

If I was to pursue a relationship with this man, I run my fingers over the hair on his arm up to the roll of his shirt, the frequencies I experience now would tone down, diffuse with time. This violence, this tintinnabula of bells. The pinwheels and rockets sensation, is very short-lived.

He moves and as his thigh edges away from mine I feel as if I'm being flayed. I focus on the simple bulge of his knee. The out-thrust limb alongside mine glows as if electrified. One tremendous paradox, this life! I swallow and stroke the Bengal yellow of the skirt for comfort.

"You're tired, aren't you, want I should take you home?"

"No!" as anchor to my drifting boat these grey eyes. In the glare there is only the present. In all the metaphysical discussions, there's never been anything but the eternal NOW.

A swearing on the bells . . . there is a magical swearing on the bells each time you love. I am marvelling at this admission when the cave within opens, and the golden light and golden liquid one begin to rise.

My breath catches at the ever old ever new sensation. Neutralizing where they meet, resting, momentarily inactive, they resume their spiral upward. When they reach my solar plexis I know what I will do.

My blouse rustles as I stand opening the buttons. He watches while I slide my underpants down and step out of them. The burn in the lower half of my body is intense.

While I straddle his upper thighs the grey wolf eyes are steadfast and would be unnerving at another time. His voice is very low and very deep, "Do you know what you're doing?"

I'm glad he doesn't give me a chance to change my mind or falter. Glad he doesn't wait for answer. His brutal mouth is exactly what I need at that moment.

Fullness against my pubic bone and lower belly stirs and grows until I think it will unseat me. I can't get close enough. As I grope for clasp and zipper on his slacks he eases upward and when I release him the phallus rises between us. Awesome velvet, unsettling in its stance upright against his belly like a young man's, I am silent before it, running my fingers softly in the groove.

"Mine," I say for the first time in my life, and I do not wonder at this. Raising on my knees I guide him into the heat within.

Within the wet he swells like a blunt hammer, the diamond clarity of a primal note shot through with violence. The energy in my spine explodes multifaceted sunset colors. "You are a Witch!"

He is a great tall tree, topped and waving in the electric current that has just zapped it at the high point of the storm. As the cone of light rises and the power sets us vibrating, he gasps. I feel the timbre of his spinal column in my breasts, the quick short breaths puffing through his lungs.

His arms tighten. I am concerned he weather the blaze and stroke his neck with instinctive fingers. Pulling back he catches my eyes for a moment and the unsubtlety of eons of misunderstood sex crash before my consciousness in a shuddering heap.

Swollen, hard, he has grown so I feel I will burst and yet I know I must contain the orgasm that would normally follow. Some wisdom tells me how to go with the circular energy lacing our two bodies. When it reaches our heads I bend and whisper, "don't try for the usual, let it pass right through us, let it flow back to earth, let it pass," I rock us both gently.

The ecstasy departs, we know interruption and separation. There is a dazed look about his forehead and eyes, as if he cannot quite believe what has happened. I smooth it with gentle fingers.

Questions are in his eyes I don't know how to answer. I'm not sure, I say in wordless response, a spell? a symbolic act in a deepened state of consciousness? I don't know enough.

He speaks first, "Come with me, I need sleep." Drawing me into another room he turns down the comforter on a large bed; we undress and lay down side by side pulling the softness up to our chins. There isn't a cautionary, bewildered, strained, anxious nerve in my entire body, I fall into a deep sleep.

Nathanial Auchin is as good as his word. Over dry Interstate, under clear sky, past Canadian snowbirds going South, I drive the repaired Pinto into New York for breakfast Thursday morning. By ten, I am maneuvering the car into its hangar by the side of the Monastery's rear speakroom.

Stretching my back in the shade of the brick wall, the turrets of the old Gregorian mansion make substantial statements against the sky. I decide not to ring the buzzer, quite yet. Settling the soft pack on my shoulders I start walking briskly, keeping to the fence line.

When I have circumnavigated the cloister house, outbuildings and eleven acres of garden, returning to where I started, I settle the pack and press the bell.

"You were not expected, Sister Mark." There is no question in the comment, the voice of young professed Sister Angela is sweet with the tacit diplomacy that does not ask. "I'll tell Reverend Mother you're back within enclosure," the other young nun with her smiles and steps aside to let me pass.

"No, Sister, I, I would rather freshen up first and then look for Reverend Mother myself, if you don't mind?" She nods acquiescence.

Muscle is full of remembering emotion as buttocks and thighs lean into the climb to the cell near the annex attic. The halls are quiet. A clock ticks on the first floor landing. There are smells of bread baking.

Sun flashes on the brass candlesticks at the foot of Our Lady's statue, her beneficent gaze sweeping the curve of the stairwell. The faint oscillating hum of Tierce, Sext and None being chanted floats up through the opening.

A door opens and closes but no one approaches and I continue the climb. Since I was to be away at school Reverend Mother suggested I move my few things to one of the cold cells. This cold now breaks on me as I open the door.

The plank bed sits under the dark, slanting roof beams, its two blankets folded as I left them. When the chair is pulled out from the well of the tiny desk opposite, there is no room to pass alongside the bed. I pull the string on the forty watt bulb, watching the cloud my breath makes. Putting my pack down on the table I remove the copy of the *Imitation of Christ* and the *Bible*, replacing them on the desk under the cross.

In the silence and solitude of that windowless room, little more than a closet, I strip; pulling the folded heavy woolen habit from its box under the bed I step into the ice-cold tunic, and layer the rest, piece by piece; for warmth, I tell myself.

Sudden poignant realization knocks me back on the folded blankets, air forced from my lungs echoing the whoosh of the straw being crushed in the mattress. I sit like that while the bells of the Angelus ring the hour. I sit past the clapper sounding noon-day meal and I sit through the meal.

Tower pigeons take to the air. Rustling wings are close as they descend to earth and their claws search the slate roof in search of footing. Smells of food dissipate. Wooden walls readjust as weight redistributes below and the first faint hum of Vespers, the afternoon hour of The Office, drifts upward.

I stand and leave the cell. It is a big drafty old house that has expanded outward in all directions. Fast on the heels of that, inevitably abrupt, come the words, beloved cradle and anchor. I am the hope of a woman bonded to a possibility, searching up and down the deserted corridors, for what? a key that will unlock the old anticipation? It is not here anymore.

I dawdle in the library; the scattering of bent heads keep their custody. I run my hand along a section of the stacks noting some of the freshly catalogued books. Leaving by the rear door I descend to the quiet, clean pantries and let myself out into the garden.

Order and care . . . I am absorbed in memorizing the placement of the trees when Reverend Mother finds me. "Nothing ever prepares," her voice is soft and vibrant. I do not kneel to kiss her hand, but take the long fingers in mine and clutch them tightly. "This," my chin sweeps the eleven acre arc, "this was where I hoped to grow old," my voice cracks.

"A part of you will." The sobs have stopped threatening, they are choking me. "Come, come to my office," her hand is firm. "I'm surprised you put the habit on."

"I was cold . . . I, I wanted to wear it one last time," I am bawling like a baby. She sits quietly watching me for a few minutes then, "You're indulging yourself in emotion."

"I can't help it."

Her eyebrows raise, "Emotions that don't have the mind's approval are mere hysterics, I'm going to the kitchen to get us a pot of tea, when I return I want you to talk to me."

Three hours later my voice is calm. "Red earth, semen, strawberries and blood . . . with the looseness of the world, that's where I found it. Since that's where the action is, that's where I may possibly weather the transformation.

"No adulteries. Adulteries were something committed before, committed in my head. I held onto ideas about myself. Those ideas were adulteries."

"I understand," Reverend Mother's voice is deep with emotion.

"Mother," mine is eager, "there is a process going

on . . . for want of a better word, of reordering information. As if, as if the body was synthesizing the things of the universe all over again . . . in order to evolve a different conceptual level."

Her cheeks are flushed, "The old forms are no longer useful, the new will come along and push them off," her smile is dazzling. "I've got to show my face at recreation, I'll have a tray sent to your cell, I don't think it wise you rejoin community."

"Leave without goodbyes!?"

"I think it best," she stands, embraces me, gives an extra squeeze to my shoulders and is gone.

Waiting for flight 311 out of Newark to Lexington via St. Louis, I look at the eight hundred dollar check. Reverend Mother returned over half my dowry money, saying I could use a stake. There is enough for a used car and I know just the person to buy it from.

Two sisters accompanied her as she opened the cloister door for me one last time. Both had their veils down and did not speak, but I couldn't mistake Barnabas' hug nor her muffled sobs.

About to step over the threshold, Sister Reginald caught me, her silent, rough hug bringing tears to my eyes.

Reverend Mother did not wear the veil over her face, she smiled that incredible smile. Then, I was walking away.

I look around with interest at the people hurrying by, faces preoccupied. A stream of people are moving toward the gate as flight 311 is announced. I feel incredibly light, it has something to do with trust and the barest beginnings of intuition.

Just as a bell is shaved to ring true, a little taken off here,

a bit there, a woman leaves a lot behind.

An old woman now, I feel one life is too short;

to digest it all requires greater perspective.

I've been just your ordinary, middle-class working woman—

if there is such a generalized, living creature—

attempting to ring true. How confusing it has often been.

How rewarding.

T.M.

Born and raised in Manhattan in the early 1930s, Teresa Mark has operated switchboards, proofread for middle management, sung plainsong in a Monastic order of nuns, run a chicken farm, worked 30 years in western health care, gardened extensively, and raised a family. She has recently retired from clinical practice to write.